D1464775

This book must be returned by the date specified at the time of issue as
the DATE DUE FOR RETURN.
The loan may be extended (personally, by post, telephone or online) for
a further period if the book is not required by another reader, by quoting
the above number / author / title.

Enquiries: 01709 336774

www.rotherham.gov.uk/libraries

Text©2011 Pat Marshall
Cover©Colleen Allen
Illustrations©Colleen Allen

First Published 2011

ISBN 978-0-9570967-0-7

British Library Cataloguing in Publication Data.
A catalogue record for this book is available from the
British Library.

PUBLISHED
by
Marshall Baker Books

Dedication

In loving memory of my Nan whose memories inspired the story, and dedicated to the latest generation of Hattie's descendants:

Jasmine, Reece, Casey, Matilda, Fergus, Joe, Leah, Abbie, Chloe and Ellie Mai.

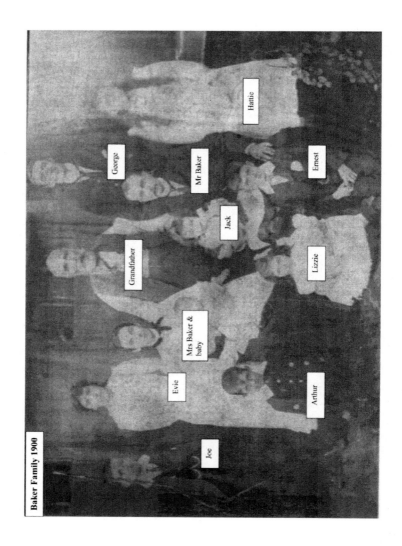

Baker Family 1900

George
Hattie
Mr Baker
Ernest
Jack
Grandfather
Lizzie
Mrs Baker & baby
Evie
Arthur
Joe

Prologue

In the murky, misty light of dawn, the young boy trudged to the mine. He stared up at the tall smoking chimneys and the great black structure that reached like a prehistoric creature, into a sky heavy with storm clouds. A man, his face blackened with coal dust, heaved a huge metal bucket to the side of the shaft. The boy scrambled in alongside other sleepy children.

With a sickening thud, the bucket swung back on its chain to the centre of the shaft, and the man began to wind a handle, lowering them into the black depths of the mine. The boy gazed upwards and saw the entrance above getting smaller and smaller, till it was just a distant pinprick of light, a single star in a dark sky.

A vicious shove pushed him from the bucket and his ankles sank into icy water. His nostrils were assaulted by an evil, sewer-like smell, so strong he could taste it. Looking down, he could just see his legs, his feet hidden in the filthy, black water.

Moisture dripped down the walls that echoed with the pounding of coal-picks, while trucks clattered and rattled along. Thud. Drip. Bang. Over and over. Tears rolled down his face as he thought of the long, frightening hours ahead and he coughed violently as he scrambled along and crouched in the foul wetness beside his trap-door.

His candle stub was burning out fast, midges flying around it in the putrid air. He opened his tin box and broke off a piece of stale bread, recoiling as he felt a rat, attracted by the food, run over his foot.

As his candle flickered and died, he was plunged into darkness and, as time dragged on, his laboured breathing slowed and he slept, an exhausted little boy of six.

1. The Haunted Room (Present day)

 The handle of the store-room door was so cold it stuck to Charlie's hand like the ice-lollies in his mum's freezer. The door creaked open, and, among the cardboard boxes, dusty files and piles of ancient envelopes, huddled in the far corner, behind an old desk, there he was... the shadowy shape of a boy.

His ragged, old-fashioned clothes hung loosely on his skinny frame. His face was so pale it was almost transparent. The cold air around him seemed to move, to glimmer and glow, like the out-of-focus reflection from a distorting mirror.

Charlie felt icicles prickle down his spine. This could not be happening, could not be real.

"I don't believe in ghosts," he heard himself whimper.

His legs trembled so much he couldn't move. He could hear the thump of his heartbeat, the only sound in the silence. Even the background noises of the classroom seemed to have faded away.

He gulped a mouthful of the icy air that swirled around him. It was so, so cold, yet there was no window in the store-room, no possible place for a draught to come from, especially a gust that felt as if it had blown direct from the North Pole.

He shivered violently under his light cotton shirt and trousers and tried to focus on the figure. The boy's bony fists clenched the lid of the wooden desk. His shirt was dingy grey with frayed sleeves, his knuckles scraped and sore.

Slowly, the figure let go of the old desk and took a hesitant step forward, never taking his eyes off Charlie. Charlie stumbled backwards. Horrified, he watched the boy float soundlessly up from the floor as if suspended by an invisible rope. He drifted until he hovered close to Charlie, almost level with his face. His eyes seemed impossibly dark and huge in the white skeleton-like face.

Skinny legs peeked out of ripped trousers that were far too short. His feet were bare and as dirty as if they'd squished through miles of mud. A bone-white arm reached towards Charlie and he shuddered as grey fingers with filthy, broken nails seemed about to touch him. Blue-tinged lips parted slowly as if they had forgotten how to form words. A croaky voice seemed to come from a million miles away.

"Charlie, find me!"

"Who are you?" Charlie whispered under his breath. Somehow, he managed to stare straight into the boy's eyes and saw tears spilling from them on to those pale, pale cheeks. And he saw his own fear mirrored there. The boy was as terrified as he was.

He felt the boy's fear, in a way that he could never have explained to anyone. As he stared into those dark and haunted eyes, he saw something else; a flash of recognition, something he tried to remember, but couldn't. Like a dream that slips away when you wake, he couldn't quite grasp that *something* which lurked in the deepest corners of his mind.

"Have you found that paper, Charlie?" boomed the teacher from the other side of the wooden door. Charlie's head whipped round and he became aware again of the rest of the class. He grabbed the pack of A4 he was supposed to fetch, and as he did, the ghost-boy floated past him, out through the store-room door. He soared to the high ceiling with as little effort as a dandelion seed carried in the wind, then swooped and hovered at the front of the classroom, staring at the children... just staring. Charlie wiped beads of sweat from his forehead as, after the cold of the cupboard, a sudden blanket of heat wrapped itself around him. He struggled to move and felt as if he were part of a film running in slow motion.

Then, in full view of everyone, as a shadow vanishes when the sun goes behind a cloud, the boy faded and shrivelled into the middle of the murky haze. A second later the blurred, fuzzy figure was gone.

Charlie's heart gave a sudden, hard thud. He was holding his breath, waiting for the hysterical screams, the stunned exclamations... something... anything... but no one said a word.

Not one single word. Although most of them had been looking up, listening to the teacher, it was obvious that they hadn't noticed anything at all. No one else had seen the ghost.

My ghost. The words seemed to echo through his mind.

After dropping the box of paper beside the printer, Charlie collapsed into his chair.

Wild thoughts whirled in his head as if a spider had spun a web through his brain. He couldn't think straight. His eyes strayed back to the open store-room door, partly willing the figure to reappear, partly terrified he would.

For some reason it felt like a secret between himself and the boy. And secrets, sacred as promises, had to be kept. It wasn't something he could explain, even to himself, just the knowledge that this was how it was meant to be. So he said nothing to anyone. He gazed around as if seeing the room for the first time.

Dappled, early spring sunlight drifted through the small high windows, casting hazy shadows on the bare brick walls of the old room. He'd heard people say the room was haunted, but he'd laughed at them. Surely it was just those Year 10 kids trying to scare the younger ones. Wasn't it?

Oh, my God, it's true. There is a ghost. But why didn't anyone else see him? Why only me?

As the lesson finished, the group clattered to their feet, eager to be out of the musty old room. Charlie's fingers fumbled and he dropped his school bag. Even the teacher seemed to be in a hurry, and soon he was the only one left… alone in the haunted room.

And now, he *wasn't* laughing.

On his knees he gathered up his spilt pens and books, but trembled as he sensed that he wasn't alone.

The whoosh of ice-cold air swirled again, rushing round his ears like a mini tornado. He wanted to close his eyes and peek through his fingers, as he'd sometimes done at the spookiest parts of a horror film. But this nightmare was real. And he had to look up.

The boy floated in the air, a luminous, white light blurring his outline. He was close enough to touch, but Charlie was sure his hand would pass right through him if he did.

The hairs on his neck prickling and his pulse racing like something demented, Charlie tried to speak.

"What do you want?" he managed at last, in a wobbly voice.

The boy looked at him with huge, pleading eyes. His arm reached out and a pallid finger pointed at Charlie.

"Please, Charlie. Find me…."

The faraway voice echoed slightly and bounced back from the brick walls, filling the room with its eerie, alien sound.

"What do you mean…find you? Where? How? I don't understand."

Then, like before, and just as suddenly, the boy faded away to nothing, only the faint echo of a sigh floating in the air where he'd been.

Pale and breathless, Charlie caught up with his friends but, lost in their own thoughts, none of them seemed to notice anything wrong.

"Hope the decorator's finished so we can move back to our own room tomorrow," he heard someone say.

"Yes, I hope so too. It's so *spooky* in there!" added one of the girls. With a nervous glance over her shoulder, she grabbed her friend's arm. "It's the oldest part of the whole school. Why don't they just demolish it?"

"I reckon they will one day when they don't need it as a spare room," one of the boys said. "Anyway, Charlie," he added with a broad grin, "looking forward to beating you at bowling tomorrow. Should be a good night, eh?"

"Oh, yeah... sure... yeah." The outing his parents had organised for his 13th birthday, the following day, didn't seem half as important now.

He had to tell his friends what he'd seen. He owed it to them to tell them. Didn't he? But how would they react? Would anyone believe him when they hadn't been able to see it for themselves? How could he describe what had happened?

Would I believe any of them if they told me they'd just spoken to a ghost who'd been there right in front of us and I hadn't even noticed? Probably not.

He stammered, his brain seemingly incapable of putting together any sensible words. "Er...er..." It was no good. There was just no way you could drop into the conversation, *Hey, guess what! There's the ghost of a boy in the store-room.*

It wasn't until Charlie was almost home that he remembered something else.

"The ghost, he called me *Charlie*. How did he know my name?"

2. The Mysterious Parcel

Early morning sunlight squeezed through the narrow gaps between the slats of the blinds in Charlie's room, making a cage with bars of light and shade around his bed. He snuggled down under his Man United quilt. The eerie events of the previous day seemed like a scary dream now.

"Wonder what he meant … *find me?* Surely I already did that?" he muttered. "Well, we're not going back to that room today, and I'm definitely not going to let it spoil my birthday."

Charlie realized he wasn't scared any more. Not one bit. In fact he knew with absolute certainty that today was going to be the most exciting day of his entire life. He'd no idea what this extraordinary feeling was all about. It sat there inside him, like a mass of bubbles fizzing and frothing.

Maybe going crazy after all, he thought to himself. But a broad grin stuck stubbornly to his face and wouldn't go away.

Suddenly, a whirlwind in Barbie-pink pyjamas exploded into his bedroom. With a speed that any goalie would be proud of, he dived to one side as his ten-year-old sister, Jessica, jumped on to his bed. Her blonde hair flew wildly, as she bounced up and down. She was holding a hastily-wrapped parcel and shouting, "Happy Birthday,

Charlie! Come on, open your present. I made it myself, 'specially for you."

"Shh," he whispered, a finger across his lips, as he took the parcel from her.

"Sorry, haven't got my hearing aids in yet," she said with a giggle. "I wanted to show you your present first."

"Wow, thanks, Jess," Charlie spluttered, ripping the paper off and trying his best not to laugh. "That's... amazing!" He held up a very long, thin and colourful knitted scarf, complete with dropped-stitch-holes.

"Is it all right?" she asked, biting her bottom lip and watching his face.

"It's great, Jess," replied Charlie, fingers crossed behind his back. "I'll be like Joseph, but with a scarf of many colours!"

"Charlie. Jess." Their mother's voice drifted up the stairs. "Breakfast."

"Come on, Jess," he said. "Race you!"

On the kitchen table, among the breakfast mugs and dishes, were some brightly-wrapped presents.

"Happy Birthday, Charlie."

"Hey, thanks, Mum, Dad. I really wanted this new game."

He gave them both a hug, then discovered a couple of great books and the latest CDs by several of his favourite bands.

As he was finishing a bowl of chocolate krispies, the doorbell rang. The postman handed over a bundle of colourful, hand-written envelopes.

"There's a parcel as well," he said, reaching into his bag. The package he pulled out was covered with creased brown paper and tied with thick white string. He placed it on the kitchen worktop and wished Charlie a

'Happy Birthday' as he carried on down the road.

Charlie picked up the parcel, then froze and almost dropped it. Around its edges shone a faint silver-blue light which grew stronger, shimmered and glowed, then flashed like forked lightning along the string and across the brown paper.

"What the ..." he began, but stopped, realising that, even though they were all looking at the parcel, no one else had said a word.

A sick feeling knotted up his stomach.

Right...ok. Just me again then. So what's going on this time? But the lights had gone. Now it was a very plain and innocent-looking package; a normal, everyday sort of parcel. But Charlie knew it *wasn't* going to be ordinary. That just wasn't going to happen.

He poked at the lumpy red blobs that covered the tight knots.

"Is that dried blood?" he whispered. Today, *anything* seemed possible.

"Charlie! That's sealing-wax," answered his mum, laughing as she passed the scissors. "You don't often see that these days."

He cut the string, pulled off the crinkly layers of paper and emptied the contents on to the kitchen table. Out tumbled a notebook, slightly tattered on the edges and covered with spidery black handwriting. He carefully tipped up a bag of old photographs and, head to one side, stared at one of a large family group. It had 'Baker family 1900' written along the edge of it.

"That's weird, they've got the same name as us."

He stared at the group.

And I recognise these people. I'm sure I've seen them before.

He picked it up to have a closer look.

As he touched it, his fingertips began to tingle. The feeling quickly became stronger and spread right up to his elbows. In spite of the warmth of the kitchen, goose-bumps prickled up his arms. His dad took it from him for a closer look. Nothing at all seemed to happen to him.

What the heck is going on? And why do they look familiar? This photo is so old, they must have all been dead for years, he thought, not quite trusting himself to speak.

His dad glanced at a letter, in the same untidy hand-writing.

"It's from my Great-Uncle Freddie."

His mum had picked up another of the photographs.

"Look, Charlie, here's one of Dad's Uncle Freddie, when he was a boy. "Oh… that's strange," she said. She held it next to his face and glanced over her shoulder at the others. "Look at the likeness. If it wasn't for the hairstyle and clothes, it could be Charlie in this photo!"

His mother's comment sent a shudder through him, a vague sense of foreboding.

He knew he'd inherited his thick, dark hair and chocolate-brown eyes from his father's family, the Bakers, while Jessica had her mother's unruly, blonde hair and sky-blue eyes.

So…? I look a bit like a distant dead relation. What's odd about that?

His dad pointed to the photo of the family group.

"That one's much older. See that tall young man at the back? He was George Baker, Uncle Freddie's father. I remember hearing how he got a medal for bravery in the Army, during the Boer War. Made his family very proud, he did."

Charlie looked over Jess's shoulder as she picked the photograph up.

"I wonder why they all look so serious," she said. "Come on, Charlie, read the letter."

Charlie frowned. *Hmm, nothing happened to Jess.*

After another quick and wary glance at it, he unfolded the sheet of paper and began to read aloud:

"My dear Charlie, Happy Birthday for Thursday. I'm a very old man now, but Charlie, I've had such an exciting life. So much travelling! However, it was always in the great plan that, on your 13th birthday, my special gift would be passed to you.

"I hope you'll continue the notes I've started. You'll know what to write when the time comes.

"Use the gift wisely and with great care. Study the photographs. Guard them well, for they contain many secrets, lots of questions, and some of the answers. Have fun!

Your Great-Great-Uncle Freddie."

"Hmm, it's odd to hear from him after all these years," said his dad "Why is he sending these things to Charlie?

"He probably wants to make sure they're safe for the future when he's...you know...." answered his mum.

Dead, thought Charlie, raising his eyebrows.

He read the letter again, trying to work out what Uncle Freddie meant. The bright, laser-like light began to glow once more and stream across the paper. He looked up to see his parents' reaction. Absolutely none.

This is too weird. Yesterday, the ghost-boy, now this strange gift from an old man I've never even heard of. Is there a link between them? He glanced at the others, but they were all simply eating their cereal and toast. Charlie shrugged and plonked down on a chair.

It's really, really strange how only I could see the ghost, and now nobody else can see what's happening to this parcel. It's like a secret I'm not supposed to share, which would be ok if I knew what the secret was.

Brain in a whirl, Charlie stared at the faded, sepia photograph which lay on the table in front of him. The family seemed somehow so familiar to him. Behind the mother, who had a baby on her lap, stood an older man with a thick, grey moustache and long white beard; he had to be the children's grandfather.

There were two girls in long-sleeved white dresses and four boys of different ages, smartly dressed in suits and shirts with large, stiff, white collars.

Charlie's restless fingers plucked absent-mindedly at the neckline of his school shirt.

A little girl sat on the ground in front. A younger child wriggled around on its father's knee. One of the girls, who looked about his own age, was slightly blurred as if she'd moved when the photo was taken.

That's Hattie, he thought. Her face became clearer and she smiled at him. Her long hair blew gently in the slight breeze that carried the faint scent of lavender.

What the...? Charlie jolted away from the picture. *I really need to get a grip. It's an old photo, that's all.*

He risked another quick glance.

"Who's that girl, Mum?" he asked.

"Hmm, let's see. She'd have been Hattie...your Great-Great-Great Aunt Hattie."

A shiver ran through Charlie. *How the heck did I know that?*

His eyes wandered back to the other family members. The wriggling child on the father's knee wore a white dress and had long hair.

"She looks as if she's trying to escape," he thought aloud.

"That's not a girl, that's Jack," said the shadowy 'Hattie', and Charlie shot to his feet, pushing the photo to one side. He'd seen her mouth move, seen the laughing expression on her face.

But that seriously couldn't happen. People in photographs do not talk. Absolutely. Definitely. Do. Not. Talk.

"Hey, look at the clock. It's time you two weren't here," said his mum. Grabbing hold of the kitchen table to steady himself, he shook his head.

Wow, for a crazy moment there, I really thought the girl in the photo spoke to me. God, that's weird! First ghosts, now pictures of people who talk...what's happening to me?

"It's a very strange start to a birthday, anyway," he muttered.

He and Jess grabbed their packed lunches and quickly stuffed their books and homework into their school-bags. In a daze, he didn't even notice when Jess wound his new scarf around his neck.

"Come on, Charlie," she said, tugging at his sleeve.

As he closed the gate, Charlie glanced back at their home, a lovely old terraced house on the corner of Atlas Street on the outskirts of Rotherham.

The swaying branches of a weeping-cherry tree looked like dozens of arms waving a slow goodbye. And there, hovering just above the long grass and half-hidden among the dancing leaves and pinkish-white blossom was a hazy figure. Again there was the distant, whispering voice.

"Find me, help me!"

The pleading eyes locked on to Charlie's disbelieving ones, drilled into them, then, in the space of a heartbeat, he was gone.

"No," hissed Charlie. "I don't want this. What are you, my shadow or what? Leave me alone."

But as he caught up with Jess, he could still hear, very faintly in the air all around him.

"Find me, Charlie. Please. Help me!"

3. Hattie

"Char…lie!"

He whipped round, hearing the panic in his sister's voice. Lost in thought, he hadn't noticed Jess had fallen behind. Rushing back round the corner, he was mortified to see her crouched on the pavement, back pressed to a garden fence, paralyzed with fear. She hugged her knees and rocked while tears streamed down her face.

This is where it happened, he realised, glancing round.

White-hot anger gripped him as it all came rushing back; Jess coming home sobbing, school clothes ripped and dirty. His fists clenched as he remembered - that creep Colin Cunningley sneaking up behind Jess to scare her. Course she couldn't hear him. She'd panicked, tripped on the kerb and nearly got hit by a car. Well, it certainly gave that idiot Cunningley a good laugh, but ever since then, Jess, poor kid, had been terrified of being outside on her own.

Crouching, he gently took hold of her shoulders and spoke clearly.

"Hey, it's all right, Jess, you're ok."

"I stopped to p...play with the puppy in that garden for a moment and you vanished," she told him with a hiccup in her voice. "You were walking very fast, Charlie."

He threw his arm protectively round her shoulders and gave her arm a little nudge. "Keeping fit, aren't I?"

Today, like most days, he was happy to see Jess safely into the grounds of her school, before walking the extra half mile to his own. Sometimes, they both got a lift to school in the car with their mum who worked part-time in a library quite close to his school, but mostly they both enjoyed the walk.

By the time they reached her school she was her usual cheerful, chatty self. She ran to join her friends, one hair-bobble lost and blonde plaits already coming adrift. Although Charlie smiled when he waved goodbye, he could not shake off the anger he still felt towards the bully and was consumed by thoughts of what he would like to do to him. *If only Mum and Dad hadn't made me promise not to interfere.*

The boy had been sent for a long talk with his head-teacher and kept late after school for a month, but Charlie had seen the spiteful looks he threw at younger children. He still didn't trust him, not one bit.

As he neared his own school gates, hysterical laughter greeted him and he stared in surprise at his friends.

"Nice scarf, Charlie," one of the girls called over to him and he noticed with surprise his colourful present round his neck. After one red-faced, cringe-with-embarrassment moment, he was laughing as well. Soon the whole crowd were doubled up and Charlie knew it wouldn't be the last he heard of it. He pulled off the scarf and pushed it well down into his school bag.

And there in his bag, among his books and homework was the family photograph he'd been looking at earlier.

"How the heck did that get there?"

He slipped it carefully between two books and caught up with his friends.

The last class that morning was history with Mr Little. Charlie liked him as he was a good laugh and a great teacher. He reminded Charlie of Little John in the Robin Hood stories as Mr Little was not little at all! In fact, he was well over six feet tall and quite chubby. He wore chunky, brightly-coloured sweaters over his dark, corduroy trousers. His curly red hair had a mind of its own and stuck out all over the place. He also had the widest, warmest smile and the kindest face imaginable.

"Some of you might have looked at the 1901 census on the Internet. Or maybe traced your family history on a website like *ancestry.com*," he said. "I bet you've all heard lots of tales about *the old days*.

"Get out your textbooks and let's have a closer look at the year 1900."

Charlie reached into his bag.

"Ouch." He jerked his arm back as once more a tingling feeling, like tiny electric shocks, ran from his fingertips right to his elbow. He stared down at his plain, black school-bag. It was positively glowing with colours around the edges like the fibre-optic trees at Christmas time.

"What's happening now?" he muttered, glancing nervously around.

"No one else can see anything strange," replied a muffled voice from his school bag.

What...? No way...! This can't be happening.

"Get me out of here!" demanded the voice.

Very cautiously, Charlie picked up the photograph by one corner and placed it on his table.

"That's better. It was extremely cramped in there," said the blurred figure at the side.

"You can't possibly be talking," whispered an utterly bemused Charlie.

"'Course I can, and it's taken you long enough to hear me," said the girl in a slightly grumpy voice. She was no longer blurred but becoming clearer by the second.

"I've been trying to get your attention all morning, Charlie. There's no need to look so worried, no one else can see or hear me."

"Are you called Hattie?" he whispered.

"Yes, I'm Hattie Baker."

"My name's Baker as well," he mumbled.

"Yes, we're… well… distantly related, but you know that already!"

"But … how… how did I know your first name even before Mum told me?"

"We've met before, but it hasn't happened yet," answered Hattie, her matter-of-fact tone of voice suggesting that this explained everything.

"What? That doesn't make sense. I don't understand any of this," Charlie muttered, his hand cupped round his mouth. "What's more, Mr Little is going to notice something odd when he looks this way. I don't normally talk to the table you know."

"Oh, it's quite all right. Honestly, no one else knows I'm here and Mr Little won't even notice you've gone."

"Gone *where*?"

He was seriously worried now, especially as Hattie seemed to be growing larger and more and more real. She was no longer part of the photograph. She was gradually changing into an ordinary girl, like all the others in the classroom; except that she was wearing an old-fashioned dress, covered by a white, cotton pinafore, trimmed round the edges with lace. She smelled of fresh air and lavender.

She perched on the edge of his table and looked perfectly at home there. His forehead furrowed into a deep frown.

"Is this something to do with the ghost-boy?"

"What ghost is that?" She gazed around the classroom. "I can't see any ghosts."

"No, the boy in the old room, yesterday."

"I wasn't here yesterday, so I don't know. Do you think it is?"

Charlie shrugged. "He's following me and asking me to 'find' him. He was waiting for me at our house this morning. But nobody else could see him. Now you're here, Hattie, and nobody else can see you. I don't get what's happening. Is it to do with this old Uncle Freddie travelling round the world? He said in the letter that he was passing the gift on to me, but I don't know what he means."

Hattie smiled and lightly touched his hand. She gazed at him with laughter in her sparkling, treacle-brown eyes.

"Oh no, Charlie, you've got it all wrong. Freddie didn't travel to faraway places. His travels were much more exciting as you'll see when you read the notes he made. And now you're a Traveller, like he was. I've come to take care of you. That's what I do."

She smiled at him again. He stared into those mysterious, shining eyes, full of warmth and wisdom. Suddenly he wasn't scared anymore. There was that huge buzz of excitement again. Whatever was happening was something very, very special indeed.

Maybe this will be a laugh, something to tell them about at the party tonight.

Hattie held his hand more tightly and her long brown hair swished against his face as she leaned forward.

"Look at the photograph again, Charlie. Go on, really look at it."

He glanced around to see if any of his friends were watching. To his amazement they were all deeply engrossed in their work.

The classroom and everyone in it seemed to be fading slightly and becoming a little unreal. At the same time Hattie was now as real and normal as any of the girls he knew.

"Come on, Charlie, I have a day off school for the Queen's birthday and I don't want to waste one minute of it. Hold my hand and look deep into the photograph."

The photo seemed different, clearer and brighter. Colours appeared where none had been before. There was an empty space now where Hattie had been standing and he could see more of the garden where the family were gathered. They were all getting larger, more colourful and more and more real. The sun was shining. He could feel its heat on his face.

Then there was a sudden flash of light…

4. Thursday May 24 1900

 Blinking from the camera's flash, Charlie stared wildly around him. Through the hazy blur of smoke, he found he was standing next to Hattie in her garden. The Baker family were grouped together, perfectly still, exactly as in the photograph. There was a strange, chemical smell in the air. The photographer removed the black cover from his camera.

"You can relax now," the man said, lifting the camera from its tripod.

As the smoke began to clear, Charlie whirled around but his friends had totally vanished, along with his school and Mr Little's history lesson.

"Whoaa... wait a minute!" he began, but Hattie grabbed his arm.

"Don't be scared, Charlie. I'll look after you." Charlie screwed his eyes up tightly, scared to look around again and hardly hearing what she was saying.

"You're a Traveller now. You can go anywhere you want by concentrating on where you want to be. Or when. All the power is in your own mind. If you think really hard about your school, you'll be back there in a flash. But don't do that yet. You're needed here first."

This is all a dream, a very strange dream, he told himself. Fear flooded through him, numbing his mind and making it hard to think or even breathe.

In a moment I'll wake up and everything will be as it should be.

He opened his eyes, at first just a little bit. The Baker family were still there, but now they were moving about. Everything seemed to be in slow motion. His thoughts were jumbled and crazy. But one thing he knew for certain. They were alive and real. They were flesh and blood people.

They were also his long-dead ancestors.

This is totally impossible. The photograph was taken in 1900.

He didn't know which was stronger, the stark fear or the sheer wonder. Unable to speak, he grabbed Hattie's hand. It felt incredibly solid and warm.

She smiled and he was just aware of her whispering, "Don't worry, Charlie. My family know that you're here for a special reason."

She gently squeezed his hand.

"One thing you must remember; in your time, nobody could see me, could they? Now, here, in my time, no one can see or hear you. Only our family. To everyone else you're invisible.

"The photographer couldn't see you, so he didn't get you in the photograph. Next time you look at it though, you'll know you were here next to me when it was taken."

Charlie stood open-mouthed trying to absorb this new information. Not only was he being asked to help a ghost, he was here with his Victorian ancestors and he was about to play the part of the 'Invisible Man'.

It was all too much. His chin quivered and his eyes brimmed with tears that he struggled to hold back. He felt decidedly wobbly and very, very scared.

Something knocked sharply against his leg, and he looked down into the friendly, brown eyes of a black Labrador. The dog panted and looked up at him expectantly. Charlie could have sworn he was grinning. Instinctively, he patted the dog's head.

"Well, at least the dog can see me," he murmured. "He must be part of the family."

A sticky little hand grabbed his and a small girl of about four tugged at his sleeve. She glared at the dog.

"Go away, Ben, he doesn't want to play with you." She smiled at Charlie. "Do you remember me, Charlie? I'm Lizzie. I'm four."

He tried his very best to smile back at the excited little girl, not making any sense at all of what she was saying. The other children gathered round, all wanting to talk and the strangeness of the situation began to ease a little.

Hey, thought Charlie, a few moments later, *that's odd, they really do seem like family. It's the same feeling I had when I first saw the photo. Sort of familiar.*

Their mother's voice floated into his thoughts.

"George," she spoke to the tallest of the boys who Charlie thought must be about 17, "You'll have to hurry or you won't have time for lunch before you're due back at work. Father and Grandfather too.

"Evie," she turned to the older girl who stood behind her, "I need you and Hattie to help me in the kitchen."

The children obeyed their mother at once and Charlie thought she seemed a lot stricter than his own mum. As she turned to him, he took a step closer to Hattie.

"Hello again, Charlie. This must be very strange for you, young man, but go inside with the others. Don't go filling their heads with nonsense though. It can only bring trouble."

"Mother believes lots of superstitions about the future, Charlie, so mind what you say," Hattie whispered.

As he followed her along the garden path, ducking out of the way of the washing line, he asked anxiously,

"Why do they keep talking as if I've been here before?"

"Because you have, but it will be in your future. Time is different when you travel, but you'll get used to it. Don't worry."

"I just don't get it. Why am I here at all, Hattie? What's this *reason*, you talked about? Is it really to find the ghost-boy?"

"Well now," Hattie replied, as she opened the back door and showed him into the kitchen, "I simply said there was a reason. I didn't say I knew what the reason was, did I?"

In the kitchen a wonderful warm aroma hit Charlie's nostrils. He could recognise home-baked pastry anywhere. It smelled like his nan's house on a Saturday morning and he immediately felt both hungry and at home. The delicious smell was coming from a strange black contraption, something between a fireplace and an oven.

Against one wall a wooden dresser was filled with blue and white dishes. Paper chains and little coloured flags hung on hooks all around the walls.

Charlie vaguely remembered Hattie mentioning it was the Queen's birthday.

How strange to decorate the house for that.

"The photograph was Grandfather's idea," Hattie told him. "We've never had one taken before."

"And I don't ever want to have one taken again," grumbled Evie. "Why, it's taken up most of my morning off and I've got dirty smuts on my best dress."

Charlie looked amazed.

"I'm always taking snaps with my mobile," he said.

"What are you talking about?" Evie exclaimed. "What's a mobile?" He knew

Hattie was giggling, although she tried to pretend she was having a coughing fit.

"Oh, just thinking aloud, Evie. Sorry," he muttered, remembering Mrs Baker's warning.

He found himself thinking about the ghost-boy again. Like him, he was out of his own time and invisible to most people. Did that mean he was a ghost too, a sort of ghost of the future? That was a seriously creepy thought.

And what do they mean about me having been here before, when I definitely haven't. As if I could forget this. And no way could something in the future have already happened, could it? That's plain crazy.

Hattie interrupted his thoughts with a broad smile and gave his arm a friendly little punch.

"That photograph involved a lot more than anyone expected, didn't it? We definitely won't forget Her Majesty's 81st birthday."

"Oh my God!" he whispered. "It's just dawned on me that you're talking about Queen Victoria!"

There she was in his mind, the short, round lady from his text book; the one with the sad and serious face who wore long black clothes and never smiled.

"I guess she couldn't smile for long enough!" he mumbled, as he watched Hattie help the younger children into their everyday clothes. She ran upstairs and was back two minutes later, wearing her own work dress and apron. He couldn't help but notice that her long brown dress had some neatly stitched patches, that didn't quite match the rest of the material.

Without being told, she took a lethal-looking knife from the drawer and began to cut thick slices of delicious-smelling, crusty bread, which she spread with creamy, yellow butter.

"Does your mum let you use that sharp knife?" he whispered. "My mum would have a fit, worrying I'd cut myself."

Hattie laughed. "Oh, I've had a good few cuts and burns, and plenty of bruises over the years, but I can't remember a time when I didn't help in the house and with the little ones, especially since Evie left home."

Charlie's eyes roamed to where Mrs Baker was slicing up a juicy pink joint of ham. It smelled utterly delicious. His stomach gave a loud and hungry rumble.

"Well, lad, I can hear you're ready for this. Arthur, you and Ernest move along a bit. Joe, you sit round the other side. I'll put the baby in the pram, as we can't have thirteen round the table. That would be very bad luck."

The familiar Yorkshire dialect made him feel more at home and Charlie realised, with relief, that she wasn't quite as severe as he'd first thought, even if she was hugely superstitious.

Evie made tea in a big brown tea-pot. She strained the tea leaves and poured cups full for everyone, adding milk from a blue and white jug.

"It's a good job the milkman comes round twice a day," she said. "It's so warm we'd be drinking sour milk otherwise. Hattie,

I should put the butter-dish in a bowl of salty water else it'll melt."

"Is your fridge broken?" asked Charlie.

Evie stared. "What's a fridge?"

As he looked around the table the rest of the family seemed to be thinking the very same thing. They were all looking at him. He grimaced and felt his face turn red as a ripe tomato as he realised they didn't even have electricity. How could they possibly have any of the gadgets he took for granted? And how could he explain that without upsetting Mrs Baker?

I can't believe I said that. If only I could go back a few seconds I wouldn't make such a prize idiot of myself.

There was a slight shifting feeling under his feet, as if the earth had hiccupped, followed by a strange whirring sound and a weird sensation of spinning without actually moving. Then Evie was speaking again.

"It's a good job the milkman comes round twice a day," she said. "It's so warm we'd be drinking sour milk otherwise. Hattie, I should put the butter-dish in a bowl of salty water else it'll melt."

Charlie's mouth simply dropped wide open. He was totally unable to say anything else and felt a bit like a goldfish, as his mouth moved but no sound came out.

No! No way! Time just went backwards! Did I do that? Just by thinking it? That seriously could not happen. Could it? He just couldn't stop the Cheshire-cat grin that grew wider and wider across his face.

"Wow! What a neat trick! Thank you, Great-Great-Uncle Freddie," he muttered under his breath.

"Come on, Charlie, get some food inside you," said Hattie with a smile and a knowing wink. I baked this bread last night and Mother made a huge batch of oat cakes this morning."

When it came to good food Charlie never needed telling twice, whatever century it was.

"Charlie, does this look like a J to you?" asked Evie, looking down at the floor, head on one side. She carefully studied the peel she'd removed from an apple for Lizzie. She appeared to have dropped it on the floor.

He threw a puzzled glance at Hattie. *What on earth is she on about?*

"Oh yes, it definitely does," Hattie replied for him, with a fond smile at her sister. "You see, Charlie, if you manage to slice all the peel off in one piece and throw it over your shoulder, it will spell out the initial of the one you will marry. And, strangely enough, Evie's young man is called James Jackson, or Jimmy as we all call him.

"But last year the apple peel said 'M' for Matthew," said Arthur, with a smirk.

"And before that, wasn't it 'T' for Thomas?" asked Joe, with a chuckle.

The quieter boy, Ernest, just smiled.

"Don't be so mean." Evie flounced away from the table. "You know Jimmy and I are going to get married."

The little boy, Jack, climbed down and Charlie saw what he hadn't seen in the photograph. Jack was a pale, sickly child, small for his three years. One leg dragged behind the other like a lead weight.

He couldn't take his eyes off the child's lame leg and Hattie saw the unspoken question on his face.

"Our Jack got knocked over by a horse and cart. The doctor says he'll never walk properly again. Poor little lad," she added, giving Jack a big hug.

"It's usually our Arthur who's the one in trouble," Hattie told him, glancing across at the next in age of the boys. "See where his finger end is missing?" Charlie stared as Arthur proudly held up one hand.

"The greengrocer was at the back door with his basket-full of goods. 'Course he came straight in, like he always does," Hattie explained. "The thing was, Arthur was going out the front door at the same time and it was blowing a gale that day. The wind caught hold of the door and slammed it shut on Arthur's finger."

Arthur grinned broadly.

"They put me in the cart with the vegetables and rushed me to hospital. By heck, it did hurt and, phew, I really stunk of cabbages."

Hattie frowned at her little brother.

"Honestly you'd think by eight he would have learned to keep out of trouble, but no, he hasn't. I wonder whatever will become of him?"

Charlie suddenly wondered that too. He looked around at the boys: poor little Jack, mischievous Arthur, shy, quiet Ernest who looked about nine, Joe who was nearly as tall as himself, and their older brother George.

Hey, Charlie remembered, *isn't George the one who was in the Army? My great-great-uncle's father… or at least he will be in the future. I mean the past. Oh, how confusing is this?*

Then he studied the girls, Evie, little Lizzie and Hattie, who had shown him the way into this whole adventure.

"I'll look on the Internet and find out what happened…will happen… to them all… as soon as I get home," he said to himself.

"*If* you get home," a sneaky little voice inside him whispered back.

Hattie's father, brother George and grandfather, also called George, had meanwhile changed into work-clothes and boots.

"See you later then, lad. Cheers for now," said Mr Baker.

George was holding the door open.

"Come on, Evie! Do hurry if you're walking with us. We've lost a half day's pay as it is." He turned to Charlie, with a friendly smile and said, "See you when we get home."

Evie tied a bonnet under her chin, threw a shawl around her shoulders and, after a quick glance in the hall mirror, picked up a small bag. Hattie explained,

"Our Evie lives in at the doctor's house. She's a nursery maid to their three children, so she normally only comes home on Sunday afternoons."

"Maybe I'll meet you again, Charlie," Evie said with a friendly smile and a swish of her long dress.

I wonder what's going to happen now, thought Charlie, when the older ones had left. *I wonder if Hattie knows more than she's telling me. Where does the ghost-boy fit into all this? Could he have been part of this family?*

It felt to Charlie as if his adventure was only just beginning.

And wow, he thought, *I'm invisible!*

5. Shocks and Surprises

Mrs Baker piled food into a huge wicker basket, covered it with a cloth, and placed it, along with the baby, in the biggest pram Charlie had ever seen.

"We have to take these things to my grandparents," Hattie told him. "My other grandfather works on a farm, you see, so they haven't much money."

"Do you want to borrow some of my clothes, Charlie?" offered Joe. "I reckon they'd fit you 'cos they all say I'm big for eleven. Yours will keep clean then."

Charlie felt less conspicuous dressed the same as the other boys, even if no one else could see him. He glanced down at the thick, white, cotton shirt, and a pair of rather short dark-grey, moleskin trousers held up by braces.

Hmm! Wonder what my friends would think about this? Laugh their socks off, I should think. Still, just in case anyone can see me, I won't stick out like a sore thumb.

"Joe, grab the front end of the pram," said Hattie, as she struggled to get it over the doorstep. Ernest and Arthur ran off to fetch their brand-new, leather football, a gift from Evie's employers.

Lizzie jumped up and down.

"Can I have a piggyback ride, Joe? Please!"

Ben whimpered and danced around in case they'd forgotten him.

Charlie waited outside the back door and looked at the garden. He smelled the fragrant, familiar herbs that grew in tubs close to the kitchen door, recognising rosemary, parsley and mint that his mum used. He ran his fingers along a sprig of rosemary and sniffed the strong scent.

"Mother grows it close to the doorstep to keep witches away," Hattie told him.

"Oh... right." *And I thought it was just for cooking!*

Nearby, another door was slightly open. Peeking inside, he noticed an elaborate-looking toilet, with a fancy, blue pattern round the shiny, white bowl.

"Come on, Lizzie, Jack. In here before we set off," Hattie said to the younger children. Charlie thought was a good idea too. To flush the toilet you had to give a sharp tug on a long, metal chain that was attached to a water tank above. He was smiling about this when, from the corner of his eye, he saw something move.

"What the ...?" Startled, he whirled round towards the brick wall and found himself face to face with the ghost.

Colour draining, he staggered backwards so fast he banged his shoulder sharply on the opposite wall and stumbled. He pulled himself back up but the ghost had gone.

Realisation slowly dawned as he gaped in disbelief at the brick wall.

"It's a mirror! It was my own reflection!"

He saw himself properly for the first time in Joe's clothes. His face was pale and his tangled, uncombed hair stuck out wildly.

How could he look so like the ghost-boy? He was quite a lot older than the boy, he realised now, but the likeness was undeniable and incredibly scary.

"That's it! That 'something' I couldn't quite remember, when I saw the ghost at school. He looked like *me* in photographs of myself when I was younger. That's what it was."

In a flash came the memory of his mum, holding up the photo of his great-great- uncle as a boy.

"This could be you," she'd said.

So I look like Uncle Freddie and the ghost looks like me. I think he must have been part of the Baker family too.

Suddenly, a shudder ripped right through him. He gave a sharp cry of sheer horror. "The ghost, it's me! That's it! I'm stuck here forever. That's why I'll haunt the school where I should have been. That's why nobody else in my own time could see him. The warning was just for me. I won't see Mum and Dad and Jess again. I'm never going home."

Legs giving way, he almost fell out of the door, unaware of the hot tears that streamed down his white cheeks. Hattie grabbed hold of him.

"Charlie, you look as if you've seen a ghost."

She threw her arm around his shoulders and searched in her pinafore pocket for a handkerchief.

"Not this time," he gasped, trying to laugh but ending with a hiccup and a sob. The whole story came pouring out.

"Oh, Charlie," Hattie gently wiped his face and told him in a voice as soothing as warm honey, "you're destined to have so many adventures, but your own time and place will always be there for you. You're so lucky. Only a very few people in the whole world have this gift, you know."

As she gazed into his eyes he felt certain she could see right inside his mind.

"You're a *Traveller* now, Charlie. Your task here may be difficult, but I'll help you all I can. You know I will."

A comforting hug and a flash of those beautiful, brown eyes, filled with concern, soon had Charlie feeling a whole lot better. Now he'd shared his fears with her, everything seemed so much brighter.

"Hattie, do you really know what's going on? Where does the ghost fit into all this?

Why does he want *me* to help him? Can I really do anything?"

"There must be some special link between you. Maybe it's your school. Or maybe he just thinks you're brave enough to do whatever needs to be done." She smiled. "I think you're brave, Charlie. You've come this far, haven't you?"

The sheer wonder of what was happening suddenly struck him and he was aware of a growing feeling of power. With Hattie on his side he felt strong again, with an incredible sense of purpose.

"How will I find him though? That's what he kept asking me to do, but I don't know where to start."

"Be patient, Charlie. He'll choose the time. And anyway, maybe that's not all you're meant to do here. Come on, let's be getting along."

They made their way along the garden path, Hattie skilfully manoeuvring the heavy pram.

They crossed a neatly trimmed lawn with a lavender bush in the middle of it. The scent of the lavender and freshly-cut grass mingled sweetly in the air; familiar smells that helped Charlie to relax.

Leaning against the wooden shed were two bikes, both polished and shining.

They're a bit strange-looking, but really well cared for, he thought, reaching out to touch the gleaming metal handlebars.

Hattie told him, "They belong to Joe and Ernest but the boys let Evie and me borrow them. Oh, I *do* love riding a bicycle. Trouble is," she sighed, "I'm always catching my dress in the wheels and falling off! Mind you, it's worse for our Evie 'cos her dress is longer than mine."

"And her corset's too tight," added Arthur, with a smirk that earned him a smack from his big sister.

Beyond the shed Charlie noticed a well-stocked vegetable garden and a little wooden fence. Chickens scratched in the soil, and at the bottom of the garden two small piglets poked their little pink snouts out of a pigsty.

"Hiya, little guys," said Charlie, leaning over to scratch their heads. He was bewildered though when Hattie became tearful and turned away.

Arthur chipped in.

"Hattie's a big baby. She cries buckets every year when the man comes to kill them."

Oh, I never thought of that. They're not like pets at all, just meat for next year,

"Arthur, just you shut up!"

Hattie rubbed her eyes furiously. As he watched a stray teardrop roll down her cheek, Charlie thought what a kind-hearted and lovely girl she was.

They turned the corner onto the main road and Charlie got the shock of his life.

"Hey! Look at that wooden post! It says Atlas Street. But I live on Atlas Street. Why, this is my own road, I'm sure it is!" His head whipped round to the front door. "And this is number 15." He looked round in absolute astonishment. "With all that thinking about *when* it was, I hadn't even thought about *where* we were. Is this really my own home? I can't believe it! It's all so different, the doors and windows and everything! We've

got a garage where your pigs are! It's so...
well... quiet ..., just those few bikes and that
horse and carriage on the road. But yes, I'm
certain it's the same place. I knew our house
was Victorian but, wow ... oh, wow...., I
can't believe it!"

"Well," said Hattie, now quite recovered,
"I did say we weren't going to faraway
places, didn't I?"

Charlie sniffed. "It even smells different.
There's horse-muck on the road, and smoke
from the chimneys too. What an odd mixture!
I think I can smell coal in the air as well."

"That's because the pit's only a mile
away."

"I know there used to be a coal mine near
our house, but it closed down years ago."

He noticed a far-away expression on
Hattie's face.

"It's good to know that you will be living in our house in a hundred years' time," she said.

With a jolt, it all came back to him. Here he was, talking to his father's ancestors, who were really just figures on an old photograph.

He stared back at the house.

What will it be like going back to my own time, knowing what I know now?

He had another moment of panic.

What if Hattie's wrong and the magic only works one way? What if I end up spending my whole life in the wrong century?

He took a deep, steadying breath. There was some reason he was here and it was surely to help the ghost. How to find him he'd no idea, but find him he would. Nothing made much sense, so he had to trust Hattie and believe that when his task was finished he would go home.

The little crowd made their way along, laughing and joking so much that they hardly noticed how far they'd walked.

Charlie was baffled.

"I really should know where I am, but I can't get used to all these fields and little country lanes. There should be busy roads and housing estates round here."

The bark of a dog in the distance, the breeze rustling through the trees, the song of the birds and the clip, clop of an occasional horse, were all that he could hear. It was most peculiar. He felt as if he was in a TV documentary showing how life used to be. They reached a small village and Charlie saw its name on a road sign.

"Well, I know where we are now, but it all looks so strange. You just wouldn't believe the difference."

They shouted, "Hello" to the blacksmith. A huge, black shire-horse stamped his hooves and tossed his head, as if impatient to be back at his work.

Nearby was a row of tiny stone cottages. The front gardens were a riot of colour as spring flowers vied with each other for the space. The front room of the end one had been converted into a little shop. A few of the women from the village were enjoying a gossip in the sunshine. Woollen shawls hung loosely round their shoulders and they all wore bonnets on their heads. Baskets, some of them full of groceries, hung over their arms. As they chatted, barefooted children chased noisily around. Some played 'tig' around their mothers' long, flowing skirts, some munched sweets from the shop.

Amid all the activity, Charlie's gaze was drawn to one little boy who was standing stock-still. His huge, wide eyes stared straight at Charlie. There was absolutely no doubt in his mind that this boy, unlike the other children around, could see him. A chill jolted through his whole body.

"It's you, isn't it?" he whispered, struggling to get the words out, as his heart raced madly out of control and his stomach tied itself in knots. "The boy from the store-room."

6. The Village

 He was as ragged and still as a scarecrow in a field. Charlie knew he must get closer, yet his bones seemed to have turned to jelly and he couldn't move a step. The other children were having fun, chasing, playing and laughing, totally oblivious to this strange little soul.

Can they see him? he wondered. The boy seemed more substantial than he had in the store-room. His skin was still almost see-through but the shimmering light around him had faded, so he looked more like a real boy, standing in a patch of slightly hazy fog.

Ben whimpered. Belly to the ground he crawled to the boy and Charlie watched transfixed as the boy reached out and stroked Ben's ears.

Aren't animals supposed to be scared of ghosts? Why does Ben seem ok with him?

Still the boy's tormented eyes never left Charlie's face for a second.

"Tell me what you want me to do," Charlie whispered. "I can't find out what I'm here for if you don't tell me."

The boy gazed intently at Charlie. There was something in his expression that reminded him of his sister, Jess.

He took a step forward and spoke more clearly. "You can't hear properly, can you? Is that why you watch my face so carefully?"

Did he imagine a slight change? A brightening of the boy's features, a hint of a smile?

"But what could I possibly do about that? I mean, it's not as if I'm a doctor or anything."

Charlie felt devastated. He would fail in his task if he didn't help the boy, but he didn't understand what he could do.

"I need to find out who you are," he decided.

He turned and grabbed Hattie's arm. "Do you know that little boy?" he asked breathlessly.

"Which little boy?" she replied, and as he turned back, the child was nowhere to be seen.

"It doesn't matter." Charlie sighed. "He's not there any more."

Still though, he had a definite and uneasy feeling that he was being watched, as if the boy had simply merged into the crowd. Those sad and haunted eyes were still close by and watching. He could feel them, sense them, following every move he made. In spite of the warmth of the day he shivered.

Where have you gone? You're here somewhere. I know you are.

"Come on," Hattie called, pushing the pram to the shop's open door. "It's a good job Mother gave me some money for us all."

Charlie stared at her, trying to determine how much she really knew.

Charlie gazed in absolute amazement at the little shop. It seemed to stock everything that anyone could possibly want and smelled different from any shop Charlie had ever been in. He couldn't remember when he'd been surrounded by so many wonderful aromas all at once. The delicious scent of freshly-baked bread and cakes overpowered everything else, but there was also a sugary sweetness, like candy-floss, a wonderful smell that he could almost taste. As he sniffed again, he caught a whiff of new leather. Sure enough, the bottom shelf was full of shoes and boots. Squeezed into a corner, there was even a rail of clothes: ladies' dresses and pinafores, men's working trousers and shirts, even items for children.

"How have they managed to cram so many things into such a small space?" he wondered as his eyes roamed the cupboards and shelves. "It's like Aladdin's cave, full of treasures!"

Noticing a row of lamps on the bottom shelf, he grinned and wondered which one had the genie in it. He turned to Hattie.

"Bet you knew this would take my mind off things, didn't you?"

Hattie's answer was a quick wink in his direction.

He couldn't take his eyes off the shopkeeper in her long black dress, frilly white pinafore and mob-cap. She scooped butter on to some strange-looking weighing scales. When the arms of the scales balanced, she wrapped the butter in layers of waxy paper.

Next she spooned some loose tea-leaves into a little, brown-paper bag. The customer put the goods in her basket and covered them with a cloth before searching for coins in her purse.

"Well, that's a whole lot different from plastic tubs, tea-bags and credit cards," said Charlie.

"Quick, it's our turn to get served!" shouted Arthur, as he pushed his way to the counter. "I want...."

"Charlie," Hattie interrupted. "*You* choose what sweets we should buy."

The shelves were packed with rainbow-coloured glass jars, a huge assortment of goodies of every shape and size. Some were strange and new to him; some he realised were his own modern favourites. Eventually, with plenty of advice from the others, he decided on a colourful mixture of mints, sherbet-lemons and liquorice.

"Let's go sit by the duck pond for a few minutes," suggested Hattie as they reached the village green. "I'll share the sweets out."

The younger children soon joined in the various chasing games that were going on around them. Charlie flopped down on the grass beside Hattie. They munched sweets and watched the ducks with their broods of little yellow ducklings. He looked at Hattie, sitting in the warm sunshine, arms hugging her knees, her long dark skirt trailing on the grass round her ankles. She absentmindedly pinched a hole in the stalk of a daisy and threaded another one through it. How he wished he had his mobile with him so he could take a photograph of her, something to take back home with him. Something to prove she really existed.

Hattie screwed up the empty paper bag, yawned, stretched, and woke little Jack who had fallen asleep on the grass in the sunshine.

"Where's Lizzie?" she asked as the others came back from their games.

"Dunno," said Arthur.

"We were playing 'tig'," added Ernest. "She wasn't with us."

"I thought she was with you, Hattie, looking at the ducks," said Joe, who had been talking to some older boys. "Lizzie," he yelled at the top of his voice.

"She can't have gone far," Charlie pointed out.

"No, and she knows not to go off on her own, in any case," added Hattie. "But where is she?"

"Maybe the bogeyman's got her." said Arthur, a wicked gleam in his eye. Suddenly, Charlie spotted her, sturdy little feet plodding along in their little black boots. As she reached them, Hattie grabbed her by the shoulders and shook her.

"Where were you?" she asked.

"Over near the big conker tree." Lizzie pointed, her bottom lip wobbling. "There was this boy who hasn't got any friends so I played with him. I turned round when Joe called, but when I looked back to say goodbye, he'd gone. Poor boy. His clothes are all torn and dirty and he's got no shoes."

Charlie stared at her. *Surely it couldn't be....*

"Did the boy talk to you, Lizzie?"

Lizzie sighed, shrugging her shoulders.

"I asked him if he wanted a sweetie, but he didn't."

If the ghost really did appear to Lizzie, why couldn't the other children see him? Was it her friendly little soul that had beckoned him? Was this another link?

Hattie said nothing, but threw Charlie a questioning look. Gathering all the children together, she began pushing the pram again, this time with a sleepy Jack piled on top, and Lizzie's hand firmly clutching the handle. Charlie looked all around, but if the boy had been there, he wasn't now.

Close to the duck-pond, looking very much as he knew it would in a hundred years, was the village pub, its sign blowing in the breeze telling the world that everyone was welcome. Outside were wooden tables and benches where a few elderly men supped their mugs of ale in the sunshine, read their newspapers and told their tales.

In the very heart of the village stood an old Church, surrounded by a low, ivy-covered, stone wall, inside of which was an old graveyard.

A huge, black crow perched on top of a high, stone cross. As they passed close by it took flight, its loud, scornful squawk scattering other small animals. The gentle breeze made waves in the long grass and shook the branches of an ancient oak tree. The rustling leaves whispered in the dappled light, while their shadows swayed in a sinister dance.

Charlie shivered again in spite of the warmth of the day. He was glad he wasn't alone there and hurried to catch up with Hattie and the others. As he glanced back across the rows of graves and crooked headstones, a sudden movement caught his eye.

He could have sworn he saw a little, white-faced boy, watching him from behind the wings of a tall stone angel.

7. Wishing Wells and Football

Just beyond the village was the farm cottage where Mrs Baker's parents lived. Several skinny tabby cats prowled the straw-littered yard in search of mice.

A speckled grey goose hissed at them, its neck arched like an angry snake, but the children ignored it, except for Arthur who hissed back. Hattie parked the pram with its sleeping baby outside the cottage door, helped Jack down and heaved the basket on to her arm.

Charlie followed the others into a kitchen that was already nearly filled by a wooden table, several hard-backed chairs and one small armchair, pushed up close to the hearth. It was sweltering as, in spite of the warm day, a wood-fire was burning in the fireplace.

"Come on in, my dears," Hattie's grandmother told them in a croaky, slightly harassed voice. "I'm getting your grandfather's dinner ready. He'll be hungry when he gets home."

She stopped what she was doing for a moment and peered at them through a strange pair of glasses that had no sides, holding them to her eyes with a little tortoiseshell stick.

Charlie wiped his sleeve across his sweaty forehead.

What a strange old lady. Wonder if she realises there's one extra today.

She went back to stirring something that smelled vaguely like boiled cabbage, in a huge pan balanced on a metal stand over the fire. Her black dress was so long it covered her feet and swept the floor. Her straight, dark-grey hair was parted severely in the centre and combed back underneath a bonnet that sat on the back of her head and tied in a bow under her chin.

She leaned over the cooking pan, concentration etched on her deeply-wrinkled face. Her gnarled, work-worn hands, their knuckles knotted with age, grasped tightly hold of a long-handled, wooden spoon. As she stirred the bubbling liquid, logs crackled noisily in the hearth.

Ugh, thought Charlie, with a shudder, *this reminds me of those pictures where witches make charms in big, black cauldrons. What is it they use ... newts' eyes and frogs' toes? Yuk! I'm kind of glad we've already had lunch!*

"Are there any jobs you want us to do, Grandmother?" called Hattie from the scullery where she was carefully putting away the ham, pie, cakes and bread from her basket.

"That's kind of you, my dear. There are the usual outdoor jobs that I find hard to do. Leave the baby in the pram outside the door. Here you are, take this to share."

She gave Hattie some chunks of toffee wrapped in a piece of muslin and a large bottle of home-made lemonade.

"Nan and Grandad always have sweets for Jess and me too," Charlie whispered.

"Charlie, will you give me a hand to fetch some buckets of water from the well?" said Joe. "That'll save Grandfather a job tonight. Ernest, take Jack with you to do some weeding in the vegetable garden."

He looked round for Arthur but he was already running away shouting that he was going to catch mice in the fields with some other boys. Charlie grinned. He was beginning to really like Arthur.

"Lizzie and I are off to the meadow to pick some herbs and a bunch of wild flowers for Grandmother," called Hattie, as she grabbed the empty wicker basket and swung it round her arm by its handle.

As he and Joe walked to the well, Charlie gazed all around him at the fields and the nearby river.

So many children, but these kids all look so happy and lively. Although he looked carefully, he saw no sign at all of the sad little face he was looking for. *What will happen if I can't find him, or can't get him to talk to me, what do I do then? I never wanted to get involved, but now I'm here I don't want to fail in whatever task it is I'm meant to do.*

"Oh, Joe," he exclaimed, as he caught sight of the well, "That looks just like the wishing wells that you put money in."

"Why would anyone put money in a well?"

Joe seemed quite baffled by that idea, but Charlie leaned over the side and couldn't help whispering under his breath,

"I haven't any money with me, but I wish I could help the ghost-boy and then find my way home all right."

Joe gave him a very odd look. A few minutes later Charlie's arms felt as if they were being severely stretched, as water sloshed over the top of the heavy, awkward buckets.

"Heck, Joe, these are heavier than you'd think."

They were both oblivious to the fact that other children, waiting their turn at the well, were staring open-mouthed at the sight of the two extra buckets that dangled in the air beside Joe. Charlie was glad to get them safely back to the cottage.

"Who's for a game of football?" Joe shouted to the others, who hurriedly finished their jobs and came running to the place in the meadow where the long grass had already been well trampled. Charlie was surprised to find that he enjoyed the rough-and-ready game as much as any of them, and all was going well until there was a shout.

"Ah no, Arthur, you've gone and lost the ball."

A gigantic kick in the wrong direction had sent the ball off through the meadow towards the banks of the fast running river.

"You stupid fool!" Joe yelled at his accident-prone young brother. "That's the last we'll see of it."

"Oh shut up, Joe, he couldn't help it."

Hattie, shading her eyes from the sun with her hand, stared towards the river.

"A girl wouldn't understand," Joe shouted back. He grabbed Arthur's arm and bawled in his ear, "You are such an idiot."

Ernest was on the verge of tears. Arthur was shouting loudest of all, as he wriggled out of Joe's grasp.

"It's not fair! I always get the blame for everything."

"That's because you always *are* to blame," replied Joe.

Hattie gave Joe a shove.

"Shut up, Joe. Leave him alone."

"Hey, who do you think you're pushing around?"

"Hey," Charlie interrupted, hoping to keep the peace. "Hattie, why don't you, me and Ernest see if we can find the ball? Joe can look after Jack and Arthur." Noticing a glint of tears in Arthur's eyes, Charlie reached out to punch his shoulder. "Don't worry Arthur, with a kick like that you'll be a star player when you grow up. Come on, we'll find it, no problem," he declared with a confidence he didn't really feel, as he walked towards the river-bank closely followed by Hattie and Ernest. This part of the meadow was deserted and quiet, until another shout rang out.

"Wait for me!"

Hattie turned round and frowned.

"Oh no, Jack's following us. I bet Joe and Arthur were arguing instead of watching him. We'd better wait. Don't want him landing in the water."

As they reached the bank, a tall, rough-looking lad swaggered towards them. Lank, greasy hair that might once have been light brown, stuck out from beneath a dirty, faded, flat-cap. It failed to hide a pair of large ears that stuck out like handles on a jug.

"Eh, you there, Clever-Clogs Baker, d'yer want a good 'iding?" His mouth curled into a sneer as he strutted around in front of the much smaller Ernest. "An' you, Shorty Peg-leg, yer sister looking after yer today is she?"

"You're a big bully, Billy Cunningley. Pack it in and leave my brothers alone," Hattie yelled at him, her feet firmly planted on the ground, elbows bent and hands fisted at her waist. Her face glowed red with anger.

"Cunningly? I don't believe this," muttered Charlie. "It's not even a common name. I wonder if that idiot who hurt Jess is descended from him."

"There's no need for you to be so horrid to my brother," said Ernest. "He's only a little kid."

His words were brave, but his voice quivered with fear.

The older boy turned to Ernest and sniggered.

"So yer sister's going to fight yer battles for yer, is she?"

He put up his fists, jeering, jumping around and showing off.

Tears welled up in Jack's eyes as the older boy smirked and taunted him about his limp. The bully fell about laughing and Charlie could see that Ernest didn't know what to do as Billy was so much bigger than him. He knew that if Hattie or the others interfered it would only make things worse.

"He needs teaching a lesson," said Charlie, under his breath, while frantically trying to think of a plan. It was, however, Ben who took action.

Barking furiously, he ran towards the boy. With a rumbling, threatening growl, he bared his teeth in a vicious, snarling grin and leapt. A split second later, the boy was over the steep bank and flapping about in the deep, murky water. He screamed for help as he'd never learned to swim. His boots weighed him down and he gulped and gasped as he swallowed mouthfuls of choking, dirty water.

Charlie stared in disbelief.

"He's going to die in there! It must be deeper than it looks or he's stuck in weeds or something. Even a horrible bully doesn't deserve that."

He untied his shoe-laces ready to jump in when Hattie pulled at his arm.

"Wait, Charlie. Look, there's a huge branch on the ground over there. We could reach him with that."

She grabbed the leafy part and tried to pull it. Charlie got hold as well, and then suddenly remembered that Billy hadn't even seen him.

"Ernest! Jack! Quick! I've got a plan. Help us pull this branch over there. We'll get him out but he won't know I've helped you."

Charlie gave a great heave and they got the branch over to the bank and into the water. It landed with a loud splash close to Billy.

"Grab hold, Billy," shouted Ernest, but by now Billy was almost unconscious.

"I'm going in," Charlie said, pulling off his shoes.

Before he had a chance to jump, Ernest yelled at the top of his voice,

"Come on, Billy, grab the branch! Do you want to drown? Do you?"

Billy started to respond and with a huge effort hooked an arm around the branch.

"Okay, we've got him!" said Charlie. "Now pull... pull!"

Charlie took most of the weight as they tugged the half-drowned boy out of the water. As he lay limply on the grass, Billy didn't know that it was Charlie who rolled him over and forced water from his lungs. Eventually, coughing and spluttering, he sat up, dripping wet, shivering and close to tears.

"Look, Ernest, what a pathetic sight he is." Charlie pointed at Billy. "You should remember him like that and never be frightened of him again. Only cowards pick on smaller kids."

Ernest looked thoughtful.

"Everyone's scared of the Cunningley family. His father's really cruel. He often gives Billie a black eye and he even broke his arm once when he lost his temper. Folks say that Billy's grandfather went to the gallows for murder. They're a really nasty lot."

Bit like their namesake in the future then, thought Charlie. *I wonder if it's true that these things go from one generation to the next?*

Billy stared hard at the thin little boy, the limping toddler and their brave sister, and knew they had saved his life. He looked down at the ground for a few long minutes. Then he raised his head.

"I'm real sorry, Ernest, for the way I've treated you and yer brother. I promise it won't 'appen again. Please don't tell nobody 'bout this, will yer?" He held out his hand to Ernest. "Shake 'ands?"

Charlie grinned. *Love it when a plan works.*

At that moment, Ben bounded towards them, pushing the missing ball along with his nose. Billy looked longingly at the bouncy, leather football.

"Do you want a game?" Arthur asked shyly. "You'll dry off quicker running around."

"Eh, thanks, that'd be grand," replied Billy, smiling through his tears and struggling to his feet.

"Come on then, take it steady. Lean on me till you get your breath back." said Ernest. Charlie was delighted to see Ernest's brand-new confidence. He had a distinct feeling that a lasting friendship might have been forged that day.

After they'd joined the others again, a strange game followed where the ball seemed to have a mind of its own. Billy stared in amazement as the ball headed off into an open space, then suddenly stopped and shot straight back towards him. Charlie hoped he would put it down to the effect of his near-drowning experience.

Sneaking a quick look at his watch, under the sleeve of his borrowed shirt, he was surprised to find that it was only four o'clock.

Well, he thought, *that's one good deed done. Now I've just got the matter of the ghost to try and sort out. I'm sure that's the real reason I'm here. It couldn't possibly be to save the life of that bully, could it? Just got to find that ghost now.*

He began singing *Ghostbusters* under his breath and soon they were all joining in the chorus. Hattie laughed.

"Well, Charlie. Sometimes a traveller has more than one task, so who knows?" She glanced at the others. "Tell you what! Who wants to go to the fair? We've got some money left so let's take Charlie to have bit of fun before dinner."

Is it my imagination, he pondered, *or did Hattie give me a rather meaningful look? Am I going to find some answers at the fair?*

8. The Fortune Teller

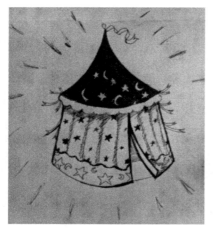

The streets buzzed with the sounds of happy people, all going the same way, for the fair was a big attraction. There was so much excitement in the air, you could almost reach out and touch it. The younger children ran noisily ahead to the meadow on the outskirts of town.

As they reached the crowded field, Charlie could smell a strange mixture of smoke, steam and oil, combined with the sweet smell of toffee apples, roast chestnuts and beer from the ale tent.

A small girl tugged at her mother's flowing skirt and pleaded,

"Eh, give us a penny for the hoopla, Ma."

The Big Wheel stood proudly above everything else, dominating the skyline. A hurdy-gurdy man in a scarlet waistcoat and shiny, black top-hat turned the handle on a barrel organ. He pushed it around on a cart that looked as if it might once have been a pram.

Lizzie tugged at his sleeve.

"Oh, Charlie, look at the little monkey on his shoulder."

The creature wore a tiny, blue jacket and a red collar with a lead hooked around the man's wrist.

"See the horses, Charlie," Lizzie went on, grabbing his hand and jiggling around with excitement. She pointed a stubby little finger at the galloping horses, which were painted in gleaming, beautiful colours. Each one had a long, elegantly-decorated pole to hold on to, as they glided up and down in time to the music.

Lizzie and Jack had a go on the swings and then they all went on the 'steam yachts'. They climbed into a model of a boat called 'The Mary Rose' which tossed up and down as if in a stormy sea. Arthur had already spent some of his money on a toffee apple and began to turn slightly green, as the waves were extremely realistic.

Charlie paused at a large booth that had pictures of famous bare-knuckle fighters on its brightly-coloured frontage.

"Yikes!"

He jumped smartly out of the way as a man staggered towards him, blood pouring from his nose, and collapsed on the ground at his feet. Shouts of rage erupted from those who had put bets on him winning. Charlie was glad to escape from the overpowering, sweaty smell of all those people crushed together and quickly joined the other children.

Arthur, quite recovered, boasted that he would show Charlie how good he was on the coconut shy.

"I'll have three balls, Mister, please," he shouted, handing over one of his pennies. The others cheered him on but his face dropped a mile when all the balls missed.

"Ah, I really fancied a nice piece of juicy, white coconut," he moaned.

"Yes, then you'd be feeling ill again no doubt, you greedy boy," said Hattie, although she was smiling fondly at him.

"Have another try, Arthur," said Charlie, whispering to Edward and Joe, before climbing over the fence towards the row of coconuts. This time Arthur took the three balls but, as he was about to throw them, there was a scuffle to one side where Joe and Edward appeared to be having a fierce argument.

As the man turned to see what the trouble was, Arthur threw the balls one at a time and with each throw Charlie casually shoved a coconut off its stand.

"Hey, Mister, look I got all three," Arthur yelled, eyes shining as he jumped up and down with excitement. The man turned and scratched his head, but couldn't deny that the coconuts were now on the ground.

Suddenly a deep voice boomed out, "Roll up everybody! Come and see the only woman with two heads! Right 'orrible sight she is, to be sure!

"Meet the jungle girl and the wolf boy, both raised by wild beasts. Savages they are, ladies and gentlemen, ferocious creatures that'll 'ave your fingers off if you give 'em 'alf a chance."

No one could resist this. As their eyes gradually became accustomed to the gloom the children gazed at the weird sights. In a dimly lit corner sat the lady with two heads.

"Hmm...," muttered Charlie, "it's strange how the second head doesn't move and the hair looks like hanks of our Jess's knitting wool."

The jungle children had dirty, tangled hair and filthy bodies. Their long nails resembled claws as they grabbed, snarling and snapping, at the bars of their cage.

The showman told the most amazing stories about these characters and how he'd rescued them. In the dim, shadowy light, and with the atmosphere that the man created, even to Charlie, it all seemed almost believable.

Nearby, and almost hidden by the freak-show wagon, was a tiny tent. It was brightly decorated with golden moons and twinkling, silver stars. Rainbow-coloured silk ribbons were tied to the top of the tent and, as they gently wafted about in the breeze, their shadows too seemed to be alive, waving, swaying and dancing in the late afternoon sunlight.

An old woman stood just inside the open door-flap wearing a sparkly, silky gown. Silver rings dangled from her ears under long, straggly, grey hair that framed her nut-brown face. She looked ancient and wrinkled as if she'd lived through several lifetimes.

"Come on, me dears! Find out what's in store for you."

A claw-like finger beckoned and a wide, toothless smile flicked across her wizened face.

"Well...," mumbled Charlie, "I'm sure I could do that. Think I'd actually be quite good at telling what the future holds."

The other children walked straight past, almost as if they didn't see her, but Charlie couldn't take his eyes away from the weird old woman. He felt as if he was being pulled to the tent, like metal to a magnet.

Suddenly, he felt the hairs prickle on the back of his neck. There, as still as a statue amidst all the activity, peeping out from behind the tent, was the ghost-boy. Charlie's heart began to race. He was barely aware of the crowd pushing and shoving around him.

"Here we go again," he muttered, "and this time I'm not going to frighten him away. I have to keep calm and get closer. I have to find out what's going on... I really need some answers."

The boy was a link with his own time and Charlie felt a strange connection with him. He'd been there at the school when the craziness started and now, somehow, he was here as well. It seemed too, they were both invisible to other people.

The brightly coloured ribbons swished around him, their shadows fluttering on the ground. Unlike them, the boy cast no shadow, as he soundlessly floated a few inches from the tent.

Charlie took a tentative step towards him.

"Why are you following me," he whispered, "even through time? If I really am here to help you, couldn't you give me some sort of sign?" He tensed as the boy moved slightly in his direction.

At that moment, the old woman shuffled out of her tent. Charlie felt as if she was staring at him. Could it be that she really did know what was going on?

As Charlie watched, the boy appeared to shrink away from her. His face became nearly transparent and he tugged at the trailing ribbons as if trying to hide behind them. Charlie was sure the old woman was about to grab hold of him.

Then, right there before his eyes, as Charlie watched horrified, the little soul began to de-materialise. First his arms and legs vanished, then his body faded away.

Soon only the pale little face was left, then just the eyes alone, staring straight at Charlie, pleading, begging, then nothing at all.

Wow, he thought, feeling goose-bumps prickle on his arms, *that's the scariest thing I've ever seen! What on earth is he trying to tell me?*

"If only I knew what you wanted me to do, what this mission is all about." Charlie whispered, still staring at the spot where the boy had been, hoping he would appear again. *Surely,* he thought, *there must be some trace left, even of a ghost? Surely he can't have completely vanished again, just like that?*

But there was nothing, not even a ripple in the early evening air. Although the old woman had gone back inside the tent, Charlie could still feel her eyes on him. He shivered, turned abruptly and hurried after the others.

He couldn't concentrate any more on the sights around him, fascinating though they were. His eyes were searching for the boy, knowing he was there somewhere, willing him to come back. But, although he had an uneasy feeling of being watched, he saw no more signs of the boy or the old woman. He felt sick with sheer disappointment.

Half-heartedly he trailed after the others as they had a last walk round the field. Suddenly he realised they had passed the freak-show again and his eyes darted all around searching for the strange little tent.

There was nothing, no tent, no old woman, and no ghost; no sign at all that they had ever been there. He felt as empty as the piece of bare ground; hollow, as if he might well have imagined the whole thing.

The children had spent nearly all of their money and the little ones were getting tired, but on the way out they saw a stall that was familiar to Charlie as well. It was *Hook-a-Duck* and promised a prize for all the children who caught one of the yellow ducks on their sticks. Lizzie brightened when she heard the man call out to them. Her excitement was infectious and Charlie began to smile again.

"Eeh," the showman muttered to himself, a moment later. "I could 'ave sworn that one o' them little yellow ducks, jumped out of the water and flew straight on to the little lass's stick." Scratching his head, he handed over a halfpenny-doll to Lizzie. "I shall 'ave to stop visiting that ale-tent so of'en."

The children melted into the happy crowd of people who were leaving the fairground, Lizzie perched on Joe's shoulders.

They shared a big bag of hot, roasted chestnuts as they walked back to Atlas Street and Charlie was surprised to realise that, at least until his weird experience, he had enjoyed the fair as much as he did those in his own time.

His pleasure was marred only by the memory of the ghost who was so desperately sad and lost.

Sighing, resigned, he reached to the bottom of the paper-bag for another chestnut. His fingers felt something unexpectedly soft and silky.

"Oh, my God," he said quietly under his breath, as he pulled out one of the silky, rainbow-coloured ribbons.

9. A Bike Ride, A Brooch and A Sleepover

 Charlie's fingers twisted tightly around the piece of ribbon in his pocket.

"At last," he whispered, "a sign that my mission really is to help him. At least now I've got something concrete, even though I still don't know what I'm supposed to do."

His head was spinning. Muddled thoughts whirled round and round, till he felt dizzy with tension.

If I was at home, I'd put TV on, or go on my laptop to unwind. Even if I go for a run here, I'll most likely get lost.

As they reached the house and passed the garden shed, there were the two, shiny bicycles. They looked so tempting now. He looked at Hattie, noticed a gleam in her eyes and felt a jolt as if their two minds were thinking the same thought.

"Come on, Charlie, race you up the road!"

Hattie tucked up her dress as she grabbed the handle-bars of the nearest bike.

Soon the two of them were cycling as fast as they could along the road with Hattie in front. The only obstacle was a sleepy cat lying in the sun. The cat stretched, yawned and gave the children a disdainful stare, before deciding to move. With a clear space ahead they got up some speed and Charlie overtook Hattie.

Neither of them knew, or perhaps even cared, that two men, staggering home after a long session at the Plough Inn, turned up at the next Chapel meeting. The Minister listened intently as they told him about seeing a girl on a bicycle, shrieking with delight and pedalling for all she was worth. The girl was chasing after another bicycle that was pedalling even faster all on its own. Both men begged to be allowed to 'take the pledge' and 'relinquish the evils of strong liquor.' Neither man was ever known to touch alcohol again.

A wonderful smell of cooking drifted from the door of number 15 on their return, and Charlie's stomach started rumbling again. Hattie grabbed a clean apron and hurried to help her mother in the kitchen.

George was engrossed in a book by Robert Louis Stevenson called 'The Strange Case of Dr Jeckyll and Mr Hyde.'

"Oh, I love 'Treasure Island' by him," Charlie told him. "I read it at school, last year. It seems strange that you're only four years older than me, George, yet you've spent the last four years working at the mine."

"Yes, I have", George replied, "but I really want to join the Army and see more of the world before I get married. Trouble is, Mother's worried I'll get sent out to Africa to fight in the Boer War and so many of our men are getting killed out there. Still, I reckon I'll talk her round before long."

Yes, you will and you'll come back a hero, thought Charlie, remembering what his Dad had said about the medal for bravery.

I do wish I could tell George what I know but somehow it wouldn't feel right. It's all in the future for him even if it's in the past for me. Heck, how weird is this? I really do know what the future holds for George.

Meanwhile, a lovely, thick, beef stew simmered away in a huge black enamel pan on top of the range. A pan of new potatoes began to boil and more pans held carrots and spring cabbage from the garden.

Charlie's mouth watered at the sight and smell of a gigantic fruit pie with a crispy, golden crust. It was keeping warm, along with a jug of thick, creamy custard, in the oven at the front of the range.

"Joe," called their mother, reaching into her apron pocket for some coins "run down to the pub for a pint of ale and don't spill any on the way back."

She handed him a tall copper jug.

Joe was soon back and they all sat down at the heavy oak table. Mr Baker, at the head of the table, looked around at his family waiting for them all to be quiet, then, raising his glass, said in a serious voice, "Let us wish a Happy Birthday to Her Majesty."

"And to you, Charlie," added Hattie. He stared at her.

"Oh, I'd completely forgotten it's my birthday," he spluttered.

They all tucked hungrily into their dinner.

Hattie's grandfather keeps staring at me, Charlie thought to himself, glancing up. *I wish he'd stop, it's spooking me out. Wonder what's he thinking?*

He gazed around the table.

"Your mum looks nice," he whispered to Hattie, noticing that Mrs Baker had changed into a clean, white blouse with a high, frilly collar. She wore a black velvet ribbon round her neck, fastened with a brooch.

Then he did a double-take.

"Hey, my mum's got a brooch exactly the same as that one," he told Hattie, under his breath.

"Hmmm…well, I know Mother's cameo is quite old. Grandmother Baker, God rest her soul, gave it to her when Mother and Father got married. Mother is planning to give it to George's girlfriend as a wedding present too. Maybe they will carry on the tradition, so it will stay in the Baker family."

Charlie fell silent, as he realised the brooch his mum wore was most likely this very same one.

When everyone had finished eating, Hattie and her mother began to clear away. The older boys settled down with books, while the younger ones argued over a comic called 'The Boy's Own Paper.'

As he did at home, Charlie picked up his dirty plate and cutlery to take to the kitchen sink. The conversation stopped and he felt everyone's eyes on him.

"Why are you doing lasses' work, Charlie?" asked Arthur with a barely concealed snigger. Embarrassed, Charlie looked at Hattie, as if she could help him out of this sticky situation. Hattie gave him one of her special winks.

"You could maybe learn a lot from Charlie," she said with a meaningful look at her brothers.

"Probably not in this lifetime though," Charlie whispered back with a self-conscious grin. It didn't seem fair, but that was obviously the way things were done. He was sure that his mum and Jess and the girls at school wouldn't be at all impressed.

As he thought about his school friends he began to feel a slightly strange sensation and could hear the start of the whooshing noise that he knew was the magic beginning again.

No, not yet, he thought to himself, struggling frantically against the whirling feeling. *It's not finished. I haven't done what I came for. I can't go back, not yet!*

Hattie pulled anxiously at his arm.

"Charlie, Charlie, you faded away a little bit. Don't go back, please! I want you to come to school with me tomorrow. You will, won't you?"

Gradually everything steadied again, as he listened to her voice.

He thought this would be the strangest sleepover ever, but was tired out after such a peculiar day. And it *was* still the same day, he reminded himself.

"It's so odd," he told her. "It feels like a week since I was in my own classroom."

Later, he and Hattie sat on the top stair, each holding a jar with a candle in it. They sipped hot cocoa and chatted quietly in the gentle, flickering candlelight. The smells of the hot, melting wax and the sweet chocolaty drink, mingled in the air with the scent of furniture polish. It felt like home... to both of them.

"We all love this house," Hattie told him, "although, of course we only rent it, but one day, when the little ones are older, Father wants to go and live in the country.

"Our Evie and her Jimmy, they've got their hearts set on actually *buying* a house one day." Hattie laughed. "Just imagine, if my own sister actually *owned* a house! Wouldn't that be something special?"

"I wonder if they managed it… I mean, if they will manage it." Charlie yawned loudly.

Just how bizarre is this? he thought. *I'm sitting here on the stairs of my own home, but over a hundred years ago, next to this smashing girl, who must surely have been dead long before I was born. George is almost certainly Great-Great-Uncle Freddie's father, or at least he will be one day. Hattie is my several-times-great-aunt. And on top of all that, I'm looking for a ghost who needs my help. Oh heck, I can't get my head round it tonight. But I'm going to learn a lot more about the Baker family. As soon as I can.*

He'd heard his mum say that lots of people went into the library to search their family history.

"Yeah, that's definitely what I'm going to do," he decided.

He desperately wanted to know what would happen to them all, but especially to Hattie. He remembered how she'd told him that he would meet this family again when he was older. He hadn't really understood what she meant at the time, but now he realised it might just be possible.

Could I somehow have a memory of something that hasn't happened yet? he wondered. *Recognise people that I will meet in the future?* He gazed at Hattie. It seemed impossible that they had known each other for such a short time. He felt as if he'd known her all his life. In a strange way, he thought, maybe he had.

She's always been there; in the photographs; in the genes we share. She's part of my past, just as I'm part of her future.

"Catch!"

Breaking the spell, Hattie threw him a clean towel from the linen chest on the landing, wished him a good night's sleep, and gave him a shy little kiss. Taking one of the candles, she disappeared into the room she shared with Lizzie, leaving Charlie alone with his thoughts.

"Upstairs, it actually looks a lot like it does in my time," he said to himself. His sleepy eyes wandered along the landing. "There's Mum and Dad's room, Jess's room, mine, and Dad's study.

"Downstairs is so different though. I suppose some of the small rooms will be knocked into our bigger ones. Oh, of course, our games room in the basement must be their coal cellar."

He knew that their house had changed hands many times over the years. Each owner had added to it, leaving behind a little of their own personality. He was quite certain though that he would never, ever, see his home in quite the same way again.

He'd seen its history, its roots, where it came from.

"And my history, my roots, where I came from," he whispered.

The younger boys were already asleep so he tip-toed across the wooden floorboards. For a moment, he stood there, staring into the mirror behind the washstand. The likeness to the ghost-boy seemed even more pronounced.

"What is the link I have with you?" he whispered. "What is this mystery all about?

When will you tell me what I have to do? And will I be brave enough?"

At last, totally exhausted, he flopped down on the high, iron bed, and sank into its soft, feather mattress.

In his dreams a little lost soul appeared beside his bed. He whispered in his ear and told him all he wanted to know, but Charlie remembered none of this by the morning.

10. The Old Classroom

A yeasty smell teased Charlie's nostrils as he awoke. Pulling on his own school clothes, he hurried downstairs. Hattie smiled broadly as she put a batch of bread dough to rise.

"Morning, sleepyhead! I've been up ages."

At the kitchen table, Mrs Baker was making up parcels of bread and cheese for their lunches. There was an apple each and a drink of water in a bottle. He gazed around the homely kitchen where Hattie and her mother worked so hard.

Surely today I'll find out how to help the ghost. Surely the next time I see this room, it will be in my own time.

You hope! insisted that little inner voice.

Most of the children walked to school with their own groups of friends.

"Hey, look at that!" Charlie did a double-take as he noticed Ernest chatting happily to Billy Cunningley.

Hattie wasn't convinced.

"Hope it lasts. They're such a horrible family, I can't believe that lad will really change his ways."

Soon the school loomed in front of them; a forbidding-looking brick building, surrounded by a high fence. A tall, solid-looking tower with a big metal bell at the top pointed up to the skies. Inside the heavy iron gates it was crowded and noisy.

Then, *clang, clang, clang*. The bell echoed loudly through the air and utter silence fell.

"Stay close to me, Charlie," Hattie whispered, pulling him along with her into the long line of girls.

"Heck, this is embarrassing. The boys are over that side."

"Don't be daft, they can't see you."

He followed Hattie into a large, gloomy room, where the boys sat at one side and the girls at the other. The windows were too high to see out of and the walls were bare, except for a picture of Queen Victoria and a large map of the world.

Charlie shivered. Then stared in amazement.

"This is it!" he whispered, "The old room of my school, the place where I first saw the ghost. And it has that strange, chilly feel to it even now. Is it possible the ghost was here back then... I mean now?"

Charlie almost expected to see his own friends there in the room. It was weird to see the boys in their drab, dingy coloured clothes and braces.

Pinafores covered the girls' dresses and their long hair was tightly twisted into ringlets or tied back with ribbons. One girl looked as if her hair had been savagely cropped.

"Nits!" he said under his breath and tripped over a bench in his hurry to get away.

"Quiet," boomed a deep voice and the chatter stopped instantly.

All attention was on a heavily built, pompous-looking man who stood on a raised platform at the front of the classroom, surveying his class and stroking the curled-up, waxy ends of his black moustache as if it were a living thing. He wore a dark suit, a striped waistcoat and a floppy black bow-tie. His restless fingers reached out and touched a long, evil-looking cane that lay on a table beside him.

"Oh boy, I'm glad he's not my teacher." Charlie muttered.

The girls' teacher was a tall, pale, very thin, lady. She wore a long black dress and her grey hair was pulled severely back in a bun.

A monitor gave out little clay inkwells to the boys while another filled them with black ink from a jug. They all took out their scratchy-looking pens and began to write.

This looks like an accident waiting to happen, Charlie thought.

Sure enough, it wasn't long before a young boy dropped a big blob of ink on his piece of paper. The teacher leaned over the scared student, a sadistic smirk on his face.

"Out here, boy. That's twice this week. I'll teach you to not to waste paper," bellowed the teacher, his face red with anger.

"Bend over!" he yelled.

The lad was pale and tearful as the back of his trousers was yanked sharply down. Charlie was stunned by the cruel thwack of cane on bare skin and had to look away.

He plonked down next to Hattie, who, at the girls' side of the room, was making clothes for a little wooden doll, her minute stitches incredibly neat and careful.

"I bet Jess would love to be able to sew as neatly as that," he said.

Hattie placed a tiny bonnet on the doll's head, smiled and gently kissed its face.

Charlie's gaze drifted back around the room.

And stopped dead.

There he was, in the front corner of the room, the same corner where, in later years, the storeroom would be. The boy turned slowly and their eyes met.

"Full circle then," said Charlie quietly. "Back in the same place."

Hattie looked up from her sewing.

"Is he here?" she asked softly, and Charlie realised that even she couldn't see him.

Those big, sad eyes roamed the classroom and seemed to be watching the children at their work.

Was that a flicker of envy? Charlie wondered. Beside the other children, the boy looked even more ragged and filthy. Then his eyes locked again on to Charlie's.

"Didn't you ever go to school?" Charlie whispered softly, taking a step towards him. "I want to help you but I don't know how."

The boy was just inches away from him and Charlie was almost afraid to breathe. As he moved even closer, he realised he no longer saw him as a frightening, ghostly figure. He saw past the small cloud of foggy white light that enveloped him to the sad young soul, who he desperately wanted to help.

But how do you help someone who's dead?

"Tell me what to do," he said.

The boy's bloodless lips parted slowly as if they had almost forgotten how to form words.

"Ask... George..." The words echoed in the air.

"Hattie's brother? Ask him what?"

At that very moment the teacher, cane in hand, took a step towards them and the boy was gone, just a hint of white haze, like the thin wispy strands of cirrus clouds in a summer sky, showing where he'd been.

Charlie slumped into the seat beside Hattie.

"He's gone again. Hattie, you have to help me find him. Please. He said 'Ask George.' Do you think your brother knows what's going on?"

Hattie looked up from her sewing.

"My grandfather is George as well. I think he might have meant him."

"Why do you think that, Hattie? What do you know that I don't?"

Charlie recalled how he'd felt the old man's eyes following him.

"I'm only guessing, but Grandfather might be able to help." She glanced around. "You go to the Iron Works now, and I'll follow as soon as I can get away without anyone noticing."

"Where do I go, though?" he asked, bewildered.

"It's not far, but you don't have to worry about that. Just think hard about Grandfather. Picture him in your mind, your power will do the rest."

"No way! I don't even know where the Works are. Still with everything that's happened already, who knows? Ok, I'll give it a go."

He tried to imagine Hattie's grandfather as he'd seen him earlier that day, tall and strong, with his long, white beard. He added a furnace to his imaginary picture. He concentrated as hard as he could.

A sudden whooshing, whirring noise came from nowhere. He seemed to be spinning in a tornado, faster and faster, twirling round and round, yet strangely he didn't feel at all dizzy. Up, up, up into the air, then as suddenly, down again.

11. Grandfather's Story

The strange noise was abruptly replaced by the sound of the Iron Works; rough voices shouting, the whining drone of machinery and the clanging and clashing of tools.

And the overpowering heat of the furnaces.

"Wow!" he gasped, "I'm here! I can't believe it really worked."

Grandfather was there next to him, shirt sleeves rolled up and his sparse, white hair and brow soaked with sweat. Charlie stared at his huge muscles.

He could be a contender for the World's Strongest Man.

Grandfather turned and stared hard at Charlie, but said nothing. He continued to pile more coal into the furnace.

"What are you doing?" Charlie managed at last, wafting his hand in front of his face and gasping in the stifling heat.

"Well, lad, I'm what's called a 'puddler'.

"Puddler?"

"Aye, that's right." He grinned broadly. "I make forge iron into wrought iron. See them wrought iron gates over there," he said, with pride, "they're as strong as any you'd find anywhere in the country. Come on, I can take a few minutes' break now."

Charlie followed Grandfather outside to a small, paved area, where he thankfully gulped in deep breaths of fresh air.

"Sit down lad, while I fetch us a drink o' water," Grandfather said, pointing to a nearby bench. Charlie shivered as the warm breeze blew against his sweat-dampened shirt. He gratefully drank from the dinted tin mug that Grandfather handed to him.

"Now lad, what's brought you to see me? I can see quite plainly there's something on your mind."

Charlie took a deep breath and began to tell his story, all the time wondering whether he would be laughed at.

I'm struggling to believe it myself, he thought.

Grandfather, however, listened intently, never interrupting or making any comments until Charlie had told him everything.

"You say this ghost-boy looks like you?"

"Yes. In Joe's clothes, I really thought it was him, not me, in the mirror," he answered.

At that moment, Hattie ran to join them. She flopped down on the wooden bench, totally out of breath.

"Phew! I've run all the way," she gasped, taking a quick gulp of Charlie's water. She looked intently at her grandfather. "Has Charlie told you about the ghost?"

She paused and her grandfather nodded. Hattie took a deep breath, rested her small hand on her Grandfather's large one and spoke softly.

"Grandfather, you once told us about your little brother, didn't you? Do you think the ghost could be him?"

"Never believed in such things, lass," replied Grandfather, his forehead wrinkled with concentration. "But who knows? As soon as I saw Charlie, I knew he was a 'Baker'. I 'specially noticed the resemblance to our Michael. Gave me quite a turn it did; brought it all back to me. 'Course, Michael never reached your age, lad."

Although Grandfather was staring at him again, Charlie sensed that he was seeing someone else, someone who looked a lot like him.

"You see, lad, my little brother and I both worked in the coal pit as trappers. Our Mikey started working with me just after his fifth birthday. I'd turned six by then and I'd been there more than a year. I was big and strong for my age, whereas he was always a skinny little thing."

"Boys of *five* worked down the mine?"

"Aye, lad, it was common practice back then. We each got paid two pennies a day."

Charlie gasped. "What! Little kids risked their lives for two pennies a day?"

"Ah, that was a lot of money back then, especially for a poor family like ours. See, our parents died of the fever and our grandmother raised us. She was a strict old soul and made us all earn our keep as soon as we could. She'd grab hold of Michael and make him go with me to the mine, when all he wanted was to escape from her and go to school."

Maybe she's still trying to grab hold of him, thought Charlie, remembering the old woman at the fair. *And he's still trying to escape from her.*

"But what could a little kid that age do down a mine?"

"The smaller you were the better as there wasn't much space down there," answered

Grandfather. "We had to open the trap doors to let the coal wagons through, and close 'em afterwards to stop the poisonous gasses building up. I took care of Mikey 'cos he was scared of the dark and the noise affected his hearing.

"When I was seven, the boss decided I was strong enough to pull the coal wagons along with the older kids, so I had to leave our Mikey to fend for himself," continued Grandfather. "He was still only six and hated it. Still, I suppose we'd have been in the Workhouse otherwise, so I reckon the old lady did what she thought was for the best."

He stopped and stared into space, then reached into his trouser pocket, pulled out a big white cotton handkerchief and wiped his eyes.

"Anyhow, one day the little lad was right poorly. He could hardly keep his eyes open. Nobody knows exactly what happened that day, but the old pit was blasted to Kingdom come. Dozens were injured, but our Mikey was the only one who lost his life."

Hattie moved closer to her grandfather and put her arms tightly around him. "You nearly got yourself killed Grandfather, trying to find him."

"Aye, I know that lass, but there's never a day goes by that I don't wonder if there was something more I could've done. Poor little lad. That old shaft was capped with him still inside it and never used again." There was a long pause and then he continued. "Worst thing was, the following year he'd have been safe at school where he longed to be 'cos kids weren't allowed underground any more after the new law came in."

And that would explain his link to the school, thought Charlie. Then he whispered, "Do you think the little ghost-boy is Michael?"

"I don't know, lad," answered Grandfather. "I reckon anything's possible though. After all, you're one of us, you look so much like him and you must have been sent to us for a reason."

They all sat in silence for a few minutes. Charlie, too, felt upset and lost for words. Grandfather, replacing his handkerchief in his pocket, shuffled away as if he'd aged ten years. Charlie paced up and down.

"What can I do? There's no way I can change what happened. Or is there?

"Hattie, if the ghost is Michael, a lot of things make more sense. But I still don't know what I'm supposed to do. I need to find out for sure if that's who he is and how I'm meant to help."

Flopping down beside Hattie, he dropped his head into his hands.

"Maybe I can find him by thinking hard about where he might be, somewhere he'd have lived and felt safe. Grandfather had said they were very poor, so that's a start. Even if we're wrong, he's such a ragged little lad, he must be from a poor area."

In his mind, he tried to see the ghost-boy in a street of small back-to-back houses and picture what it might mean to live in a slum. Vaguely, as if from very far away, he heard Hattie calling,

"Wait, wait for me, Charlie, I'll come with you."

But he was already inside the whirlwind and the strange whooshing sound was filling his ears.

He was on his way to get some answers from a boy called Michael.

12. Search For The Ghost

 Charlie screwed up his nose as a pungent smell, like a badly-blocked drain, burned the back of his throat. The narrow cobbled street was filled with shabby little houses that seemed to lean on each other for support.

He had no idea where he was and realised, for the first time, that he was on his own. Nobody could hear or see him and no one knew he was there.

Was this where Michael had lived? Where was he now?

A mangy old dog snarled near his feet. It had found a scrap of stale bread on the road and Charlie realised with horror that a tiny girl had grabbed it and put it in her own mouth. Nearby a young boy scratched himself till his arms bled.

"Oh, this is gross," Charlie muttered, aware of the pervading sense of despair that surrounded him.

An old woman opened her front door and emptied a chamber pot into the gutter, right beside him.

"Yuk!" Charlie jumped to one side. The woman pulled her grey, woollen shawl tighter round her shoulders, over her stained and torn black dress. She turned and smiled a broad, toothless smile at her neighbour and Charlie saw that she wasn't old at all, probably not much older than himself. Nearby a baby cried in a pram, and was rocked by a small girl, who stood on her toes to reach the rickety handle.

A loud clattering sound startled him as a horse-drawn carriage passed hastily through the smelly street. The wealthy passenger reached out, holding a lace handkerchief to his face and threw a few pennies into the flat cap of a beggar who sat on the cobbles. The man had only one leg, and Charlie realised that what was in his cap would be all that he had to survive.

He wandered up and down the street for what seemed like hours, studying the faces of the children, searching for the one he might be able to help. The one who had not survived this terrible place.

Girls sang skipping songs and played hopscotch. Boys whooped and fought and yelled. A few played marbles with little stones.

Skinny children with filthy faces and bare feet danced on the dirty cobbled street. Two of them formed an arch with their arms and the rest trouped under it. As they reached the end of their song, Charlie heard a familiar, faraway, almost metallic voice echoing their words. *The big ship sails on the ally ally o.* He tried desperately to work out which direction it was coming from.

"Where are you, Michael?" he called aloud but the alien sights and sounds seemed to mock him. Charlie felt damp warmth on his cheeks, tears of frustration and anger that there was nothing he could do to help these children, at least all but one of them. And he had no idea where that one was, or what that help was going to consist of.

"Don't look so worried," said a voice at his side. Charlie nearly jumped out of his skin before realising that it was Joe. Ben barked and jumped up to lick Charlie, as if he'd known him forever.

"Joe, what're you doing here?"

"Our Hattie wanted me to find you 'cos she was worried. Ben was hanging around the school yard for some reason as well today. He tracked you down, the clever old boy."

Charlie dawdled along beside Joe, his eyes wandering from one group of children to another. The shrill voice of a small girl drifted over to Charlie.

"Don't you put yer tongue out at me, our 'arry, else I'll tell on yer."

His dark mood lifted a little and he smiled at a tiny boy, nose streaming and jacket sleeve almost torn out, being pulled forcibly along, by his sister who was only a little older than him.

"Hey, wait for me!"

Charlie whipped round to find Hattie rushing up to them.

"You're making me do a lot of running today," she gasped. "I thought I'd better come and find you... make sure you didn't get yourself into trouble. You didn't find him then, Charlie?"

He shook his head and gave a last sad look around.

She gave his arm a squeeze. "Come on then, let's go home."

Ben, a heavy chunk of wood in his mouth, trotted proudly along beside them. Once they got away from the built up area, the children took turns at throwing the wood for him to fetch. Ben was like a streak of lightning, chasing after it and bringing it back. As he waited expectantly for the next throw, his body quivered. His tail thrashed from side to side, and his bright, eager eyes followed their every move.

Joe ran on a little way ahead with Ben, and Hattie turned to Charlie.

"After you go home, will you think about us sometimes?"

"'Course I will," he replied, wondering why Hattie was talking like this. He hadn't even found out yet what his quest was, let alone completed it. She seemed so sad that he put his arm around her shoulders and, for a moment, she clung tightly to him.

"We will meet again, Charlie, in your future," she began to explain.

An animal yelped in the distance. Charlie's head shot up at the sound of a creature in distress.

"Hey, can you see Ben?" yelled Joe. "I threw the stick over by the pond, but he's gone hurtling off into the undergrowth and now I can't see him at all. Do you think he's caught in a trap or something?" Joe was struggling to keep the rising panic out of his voice. "Come on, quick, run!"

They searched high and low, shouting as they went, but Ben was nowhere to be found and now they couldn't even hear the yelping.

"He's got to be round here somewhere," gasped Charlie, fighting his way through the tangle of weeds, spiky yellow, gorse bushes and thorny brambles that in places were taller than him. "He can't have just vanished. Joe, you go to the left of the pond, I'll go to the right. Whistle if you find him. Hattie, follow me. I'll stamp a path through for you."

Charlie pulled and tugged, not even noticing the scratches on his arms or the rips on his clothes.

He came to an abrupt halt as he noticed a light about fifty yards in front of him. He stared, arm raised above his eyes, trying to focus on the bright, white light that was shimmering and glowing with flashes of blue running through it. It reminded him of the strange parcel and the lights that had appeared on his school-bag.

Was that today or yesterday? he wondered vaguely.

Then he saw the boy.

He was at the very centre of the light. This time, with no hesitation at all, heedless of the thorns, Charlie forced his way forward.

He knew he had to follow his gut-feeling, certain that this was part of his destiny.

He remembered how Ben had gone to the boy before. Had the ghost somehow led Ben to this place? He looked over his shoulder, but Hattie, hampered by her long dress, had fallen behind.

A few feet away from the boy, he heard a faint whimpering sound again, but still it seemed to come from a long way off.

"Where's Ben? Please help us," begged Charlie, realising that he was asking the same that the boy had asked of him. Then he stared directly at the boy.

"Are you Michael?"

The boy nodded slowly and pointed downwards.

"What is it?" asked Charlie, following the boy's gaze, and pulling aside the long, choking weeds. He yelled out loud as he saw a huge, gaping hole in the ground, right in front of him, a yawning, black chasm that seemed to go down forever. Leaning over the edge, he felt some brickwork around the inner part, but inside it was pitch black.

He could hear the whimpering coming from deep down in the earth and called out, "Hang on, Ben, we'll get you out."

Putting two fingers to his mouth, he gave a piercing whistle.

Joe came running, stumbling through the overgrown, thorny tangle.

"Stay, Ben. Keep still." Charlie tried to encourage the dog.

Joe reached them and stopped dead, staring down at the ground. He didn't seem aware at all of the light or the boy.

"Oh God, Charlie, it's an old mine shaft, a disused one. They go down forever. "Hattie," he yelled, looking over his shoulder, "run and get help and a rope." He leaned over into the gaping, black mouth. "Ben must have fallen on to a ledge and that's saved him. But if he moves, he's had it.

"Look, Charlie, there's a sort of rope-ladder inside. I'm going down."

"Maybe we should wait for help to come. It doesn't look at all safe," said Charlie, but Joe was already on his way down.

Charlie looked up and saw Michael watching intently.

Suddenly he understood.

13. Michael

"This is it, isn't it, the old mine shaft where you were trapped?"

Charlie realised that not only had this evil place claimed Michael's life, but could take Joe and Ben as well if he didn't do something fast. And he knew he would need to be braver than he'd ever been before.

"Michael, listen, I need your help," he told the boy. "I have to get down the mine; not *now*, but on that last day you were there, the day you were trapped. Show me what happened. Please."

He reached out to the ghost-child.

"Come with me, Michael. I can't do this on my own. I need you with me."

He had a split-second's clear vision of this little boy, lying at the bottom of that hole when everything around them began to change.

The boy held his hands out towards Charlie, and, as they touched, what had been gossamer-like, without substance, became human flesh. Hands grasped hold of his; small hands used to hard physical work, with scraped knuckles and calloused palms.

A faint, rumbling sound grew louder as if a great storm was approaching. The sky seemed threatening and so black, it was near impossible to see anything. It felt like the dead of a stormy night. Then, like dawn after darkness, a dim, misty light surrounded them.

The pond and undergrowth were gone. In their place were buildings, tall, smoking chimneys and a great, black structure, reaching up like a gigantic prehistoric creature, into a murky sky, still heavy with storm clouds. Michael was there beside him, but was most definitely a real live boy, albeit still skinny, small and very pale.

A man was heaving a big, metal bucket to the side of the shaft, and Michael pulled Charlie with him, as he climbed into it, along with two other little boys and an older one. With a sickening thud, the bucket swung back on its chain to the centre of the shaft, and the man began to wind a handle, to lower them into the black depths of the mine. Charlie looked up and saw the entrance above getting smaller and smaller till it was just a distant pinprick of light, a single star in a dark sky, and then they were at the bottom.

The boys jumped out of the bucket, and Charlie felt his ankles sink into icy cold water. He choked and tried not to vomit as his nostrils were assaulted by an evil, sewer-like smell, so strong that he could almost taste it. Looking down, he could just make out his trouser legs, his feet hidden in the filthy, black water. The older boy lit three short stubs of candle which he thrust at the young boys.

"'ere y'are. And there's no more when them's gone. You lot get to yer positions and tell them kids who're finishing their shifts to get back 'ere sharpish afore the bucket goes back up without 'em."

He sent them on their way with a vicious shove. Horrified and scared to death, Charlie followed Michael along the low, narrow tunnel. Mostly he had to go on his knees in the cold, black water, as the roof was so low. At the lowest points they both crawled on their stomachs.

The other little boys each found their own trap door, but Michael's was furthest along, right at the end of the dark tunnel. There was no room anywhere to stand upright. Charlie felt a pain shoot up the back of his legs from cramp. His back ached with stooping and his shoulders kept smashing into the stony walls. The dust gritted his eyes, so he wanted to screw them tightly shut, but even the flicker from the candle stubs was better than nothing. He coughed violently, his lungs unable to cope with all the muck that he was breathing in.

I can get out any time I want and think myself back home, he reminded himself, *but I can't do it. I just can't.*

In the occasional patches of dim light from the miner's lamps, he could see near-naked men, some lying on their sides in the wet, others bent nearly double. They hammered at the walls with picks, scratching and banging to get the coal out. As they managed to force chunks of coal from the seam in the rock, it was picked up by older children who struggled to haul the heavy lumps into trucks. Underneath all the muck and dust that blackened their faces and bodies, some of these were girls, little older than himself.

At the end of the tunnel, Michael sat down cross-legged, coughing violently, in the filthy wetness beside his trap-door. Suddenly there was a loud, rumbling, rattling noise as a coal truck trundled its way along the tracks. It was pulled by a boy, bent double and attached to the truck by a chain around his waist.

The boy yelled at Michael, "Hurry up! Get that door open! Hurry! Hurry!"

Michael pulled sharply on a piece of rope and the door creaked open, then thudded closed, when the truck and its heavy load had passed through.

In a short flash of dim light, Charlie was aware of wooden beams, like pillars, which, he supposed, held up the roof of this mine. They hardly looked strong enough to support all that weight, and he knew with icy horror, that he, as well as Michael, might never see daylight again.

He felt moisture dripping down the walls, adding to the disgusting, filthy, wet mess that they were forced to crouch in.

Nothing could have prepared him for the noise that assaulted his ears, the constant dripping of the water, the pounding of coal-picks hitting the walls, the clattering and rattling of the trucks. Constantly, thud, drip, bang, echoing over and over. How did they stand this, hour after hour, day after day after day? No wonder these children were deafened.

Michael's candle stub was burning out fast, midges flying around it in the putrid air. In a croaky voice, he told Charlie that they should eat their food before the light went out totally. Charlie was moved to tears when the little boy opened his tin box and broke his piece of dry, stale bread, offering half to him.

Before it reached their mouths though, Charlie felt something run over his foot and recoiled in horror.

Rats, fighting for their own survival, were attracted to the meagre food. He cringed as he forced himself to put the bread in his mouth.

Michael gave him a drink of water from a metal bottle and told Charlie that he was one of the lucky ones. Some of the children had no food or fresh water all the long day. Some, he said, were so lonely that they made pets of the rats and tried to tame them. Charlie shuddered violently.

Nearby a girl cried out, as she was beaten for falling over.

Charlie knew that these trap doors were there to stop clouds of poisonous gas from building up and causing explosions.

Grandfather had told them that, but he could never, in his wildest imagination, have realised the suffering of the children who operated them.

As the candles burned out, they were plunged into total darkness and, as time dragged on, he noticed that Michael's laboured breathing was slowing and he yawned constantly.

What a filthy and frightening place this was. Yet, in spite of the deafening noise, Michael was soon curled up fast asleep, an exhausted little boy of six. Suddenly, there was a rumbling, not quite the same as before. He could faintly make out the shape of a coal truck approaching. No one was guiding it and it was gathering speed on the slight slope of the track.

Charlie got ready to pull the door open, but, just before it reached them, the truck veered sideways. With a hideous thud, it collided sharply with one of the wooden props. The wood started to splinter and, as it crumbled, rock and stone began to fall from above. Michael, deafened, sick and exhausted, slept on as more and more of the wooden props collapsed and fell around them. The roof itself seemed to be falling in. He shook Michael violently till he woke. Then he gasped in horror as one of the wooden beams fell towards them, and landed across the boy's legs, trapping him firmly beneath it.

"Get out, Charlie, get out, go while you can," cried the boy weakly, but Charlie, terrified as he was, knew now, without doubt, that this was the reason he was there, the reason for everything that had happened. He had no choice. He had the power to escape, but he couldn't leave Michael behind. He had to save him. This was an accident that should never have happened.

Crouching lower, he got his shoulder under the heavy beam, wondering why it had looked so fragile before. With an almighty shove, he heaved it off the boy and pulled him away from the worst of the falling rocks.

"Thank God for that," Charlie shouted to him. "Come on, everyone else has gone. We'll be all right now. Just need to reach the shaft and we're out of here."

Although frightened, bruised and dazed, Michael was able to pull himself along. He led the way as, sweating and breathing hard, the two boys crawled and clawed their way back towards the shaft and the way out of the death-trap.

Far, far above, and unknown to the two boys, the billowing storm clouds had covered the sky with a threatening blanket of blackness. A loud rumble of thunder filled the air with foreboding. Sudden, torrential rain began to destroy everything in its path.

Hailstones rattled, like stones hurled from an angry sky, sending people and animals scurrying for shelter. Flashes of lightning cracked open the sky and lit up blackened trees and broken bridges. The wind roared and howled as the ravaged earth transformed into a sheet of destructive, raging water.

Deep in the mine, the two boys were suddenly aware of the pounding of rocks hurtling down around them, as if flung by giant hands.

Charlie tried to protect his head with his arms. He yelled for Michael, but his voice was completely lost in the angry, raging torrent of falling stone. Reaching all around him in the darkness, he felt for the boy.

Michael wasn't there.

There was a solid wall of rock in front of Charlie, cutting him off from the exit shaft.

Water gushed into the mine. The narrow space where he crouched would be submerged in moments. There was nowhere to go.

Charlie was alone and he was going to die.

14. Trapped

As his eyes slowly became accustomed to the dark, Charlie realised that the rock-fall had separated him from Michael; Michael, the only one who knew the way out of this hell. The stinking water already covered his legs, and the roof of the mine seemed to be getting closer and closer to his head. He vaguely noticed things floating past him, lamps and tools dropped by the miners; greasy paper that had contained their meagre lunches of bread and dripping; scraps of newspapers brought to read while they ate. Even a miner's jacket, looking too much like a dead body in the dismal light, drifted past.

He grabbed a passing lamp, then realised it was ruined.

After the earlier roaring, an uncanny silence had descended. He felt as if he were the last person alive in the whole world. There seemed no hope at all. His heart lurched and sheer terror threatened to engulf him.

Suddenly he heard a familiar voice. The soft, clear tones may have been only in his imagination, but he knew who was calling to him.

"Come on, Charlie. Dig. Dig. You can do this."

"Hattie, where are you?" he called. He knew she wasn't there, at least not physically.

Not even born yet, he realised with a jolt. But her words, wherever they came from, sparked hope inside him.

"Michael," he yelled as loudly as he could. "Can you hear me?"

As he called, he clawed with his bare hands at the rocks that separated them. Suddenly, he heard it; a faint, scrabbling sound and a weak voice from the other side of the rock-fall. Michael was alive!

"Thank God. Come on, Michael, dig your way out. Dig."

Frantically Charlie scraped and tugged, and moved a few pieces of rock. Blood poured down his arms where he had gashed his fingers on sharp edges. His knuckles were scratched and bleeding, and several finger nails were torn away.

The water was rising. He knew it was only a matter of time, maybe just a few minutes, before he would run out of air that was fit to breathe. After what felt like hours, there was a hole in the wall of rock large enough to put his fist through.

Frightened little fingers, as rough and blistered as his own, grabbed his hand tightly. Michael's hand felt so small that tears coursed down Charlie's face and his efforts were renewed. He had to save the life of this little boy, at all costs. But which way should they go?

"We can't get out this way, Charlie," sobbed Michael. "We can't get back to the shaft where the bucket is. It's blocked. We're not going to make it. Charlie, we're going to drown. The water's up round my shoulders."

"Michael, listen to me. We *are* going to get out. There's no way I'm going to let us both die in this place." Charlie shouted through the hole, "Think, Michael. Think! Is there another way out?"

"There's the old shaft. It's on the side you're on. They used to send coal up that way, but it's not used now. There's no bucket though to take us up. I don't even know if it's been sealed at the top."

"Right, come on! It's our only hope," answered Charlie.

He choked violently as his mouth suddenly filled with the disgusting, filthy water that lapped around him. He shuddered as a dead rat floated inches from his face. Both boys struggled to move another piece of rock. And then Michael was able to squeeze through.

Charlie could only just feel the bottom of the mine below him now, and the roof seemed to be directly above his head. Terror took hold of him and for a second he could not move. The desperate urge to think himself to safety was overpowering, but how could he leave Michael behind? He felt the boy grab hold of him as he struggled to keep his head above water and the decision was made. They would get out together or not at all.

Almost on their sides, panting in the tiny space that was left, the two inched their way slowly along the coal seam. Wooden beams that had once propped the walls up, floated now in the water, snapped in bits like matchsticks. It all looked so fragile and so very unsafe.

Charlie was sure that the whole pit could collapse at any moment. At last, Michael, one arm firmly round Charlie's neck, pointed with his free hand.

"Look, there it is, the old shaft!"

Charlie's heart sank right down into his sodden shoes. The hole seemed to go straight vertically upwards. There was no way they could climb up. Round the base of the shaft was some kind of brickwork, but how could they even get a foothold when they could barely see what they were doing?

"There used to be a rope ladder inside," Michael told him, "I think we could climb up that."

If it's not rotted away, Charlie thought, but said nothing. To his immense relief, he felt the rope a few feet up. He gave a sharp tug and it stayed in place.

He pushed Michael upwards till he could get his feet on to the bottom rungs, and then pulled himself up behind him. It was incredibly cramped and dark as they began, painfully and slowly, to inch their way up, rung by rung. Every muscle in Charlie's body screamed in agony and he wanted desperately to stop and rest. He glanced down the shaft, and knew, whatever lay ahead of them, there was no going back. The evil, putrid water was already lapping just below his feet. They had to get out this way, or not at all.

Once more, he could hear Hattie's voice inside his head. "Come on, you can do it, Charlie, keep going!"

Michael stopped climbing. Charlie realised that they had reached a little ledge and were able to rest for a moment. But every second was precious as the water was rising fast right behind them.

He looked upwards.

"Look, Michael, there's a light. We're going to make it!"

The tiny pinprick of brightness got larger and closer.

As they approached the longed-for daylight, they grinned at each other as they summoned up their last ounce of energy for the final push to safety.

Then the whole roof of the mine collapsed.

15. Return

Charlie gradually became aware of his surroundings again. Everything seemed to be in slow motion, distant and unreal. The darkness had gone, it was warm and bright. Voices came from far away and made no sense at all. He shook his head to clear the fog in his brain, trying hard to focus on where he was… and *when*.

His head whirled with crazy, jumbled thoughts. He could vaguely see his school-friends but they didn't seem quite real. He could see Mr Little's mouth moving, but couldn't make out the words.

What had happened? Was Michael safe? As his head began to clear, he felt a surge of hope. He was back and alive. Surely, if he got out, Michael must have as well. So, he wondered, was this the reason he'd travelled through the years? Had he really fulfilled his quest?

But what about Joe and Ben? I left them down that mine, he remembered, with a feeling of panic. He remembered the rope ladder and the ledge that seemed to have stopped Ben's fall. *Was it really the same shaft? The same ledge? And Hattie! I didn't even get to say goodbye.*

He looked on his desk at the photograph that had started it all. The colours were slowly fading and the figures were becoming still and lifeless again. But just before the last remnants of life and colour vanished, Charlie could have sworn that Hattie looked straight at him, smiled and nodded her head. Then, with a cheeky little wink, she faded away, and became the blurred figure once more.

He stared at the photo and remembered what she had told him.

"Next time you look at it, you'll know you were here, next to me."

As he looked around him now, everything in his own time was exactly as it had been before it all began. It all seemed so impossible, so completely inexplicable, that he wondered if, in fact, he had dropped off to sleep and the whole adventure had been a dream.

His hands showed no sign at all of rope-burns or cuts. There was no hint of the blood, wetness and filth that had covered him.

So did it really happen at all? he wondered. He looked down, running his hands over his clothes.

And then he found it, right there in his shirt pocket, the tiny doll that he knew Hattie had slipped in there as a gift for Jess.

How else could it be there? Where else could it have come from? Who else could have sewn such care and love into every stitch?

It really happened! It really did!

"Happy Birthday, Charlie," called a friend, as they all trooped out of the classroom. Startled and dazed, Charlie realised it was only lunchtime, and it was still his birthday. How could he possibly have done so much? Had time here really stood still?

Everything was exactly as it ought to be.

There was one thing he had to do before he left school later that day. He found the caretaker and asked if he could have the key to the old room as he'd left something there. *Or someone,* he thought to himself. He took a deep breath before he opened the door to the old classroom. No one ever did this. No one came in here alone. What was he going to find? Would the room still be as creepy as before?

"Have I succeeded in my quest?" he whispered, as he slowly turned the key and walked into the room. He gazed around, imagining this room as he had seen it a little while ago.

Was it his imagination, he wondered, or did the room feel different? The store-room door beckoned him, as surely as if someone stood there calling. He opened the door. Flicked on the light.

The dusty old desk, which still stood at the rear of the store-room, looked like the ones he'd seen in Hattie's classroom. Maybe it had been kept all those years deliberately, maybe just forgotten.

"Michael," he whispered softly, "are you here?"

He knew, though, with every fibre of his being, that Michael wasn't there. There was no freezing wind, no icy draught, nothing at all. It was just a cluttered, slightly musty, old store-room.

He ran his hand slowly over the old desk. The wood was worn, rough and uneven, but he felt something else. He stared hard as his fingers traced the letters, carved deeply into the wood.

MICHAEL BAKER

So you did go to school after all. I really did get you out of that mine.

Charlie smiled broadly as he put out the light, then closed and locked the door.

16. Afterwards

After school that day, Charlie and some of his friends went out for a birthday meal and a game at the bowling alley. Jess and some of her friends came too.

Halfway through the game, Jess stepped up for her turn to bowl. The heavy ball slipped out of her small hand and rolled the wrong way. She turned to fetch it back, but a boy reached it first and picked it up for her. She smiled brightly up at him and said, "Thank you."

She turned back to face Charlie.

"Oh, that Colin Cunningley is such a nice boy. He always helps me at school too, and tells me if there's something I don't hear."

Charlie stared.

"I thought you were … eh… just a bit… eh… scared of him, Jess," he said hesitantly.

"Why on earth would I be scared of him?" Jess asked, with a puzzled expression. "He's a really kind boy. He always has been, ever since my first day at that school."

Charlie was totally lost for words.

I've done it again! Billie must have grown up and raised his own family in a more loving way and it carried on like that through the generations. Oh, this is really something! I've changed history! Wow!

Hesitating for a moment, he took the tiny doll from his pocket and gave it to Jess.

"Here's a little present for you, Jess. Something a friend made and thought you might like."

Jess held the small figure carefully in her hand, stroking its beautifully made clothes. A smile lit up her face and she pointed across to the far side of the room.

"She made it, didn't she, Charlie?"

Stunned, Charlie whipped round. There was Hattie, leaning against the wall, eyes twinkling with delight.

"You're here," he whispered, hurrying to her side. "Jess could see you too."

"She won't remember that, but I had to come and wish you Happy Birthday properly."

"Did I really do all that I think I did?" he asked.

Hattie laughed and Charlie could see that she was already beginning to fade away.

"You'll find what you want to know, Charlie."

Great-Great-Uncle Freddie's words suddenly popped into his mind.

"Study the photographs, for they contain many secrets, many questions, and some of the answers."

He certainly had questions.

"Will I see you again, Hattie?" An enigmatic smile was the only reply as Hattie slowly disappeared and Charlie was left staring at the wall.

"Come on, Charlie. Stop daydreaming. Mum wants to light the candles on your cake."

Charlie sighed and followed his sister.

When they got home, he took the parcel of photographs up to his room. There was something quite familiar about the very first one he picked up.

"Yeah!" he cried out loud, punching the air with his fist. There, as clear as day, was a tall, proud-looking young man in old-fashioned army uniform. Beside him stood an equally proud younger boy, whose hand rested on the head of a black labrador dog. It was George, Joe and Ben.

Charlie grinned happily.

So they were all right after all. I wonder if this one was taken when George received his medal. Oh well done, George! And well done Joe, for rescuing Ben. And Ben, it was you who found the mine shaft! Wow!

Saturday morning arrived and Charlie's mum was going to work.

"Can I come with you, Mum? I want to do some research."

He knew that to make a family tree would be a long and difficult job, but wanted to make a start.

"I think Nan and Grandad might be able to help me fill in some gaps," he told his mum. "First, I want to see what I can find out about our house."

His mum showed him some websites that would help. A few minutes later, there, on the screen in front of him, was the information he wanted.

The whole row of houses had indeed been built by the Coal Board for their workers. Number 15 had been rented to the Baker family until 1905, when it was sold. The first owners of the house had been Mr and Mrs James Jackson.

Charlie just restrained himself from shouting out loud, but was absolutely thrilled with his discovery.

Hattie's family must have moved to the country after all and Evie and Jimmy bought the house. So their wish to buy their own home came true, after all. And they bought the very house that they all grew up in... and that I live in now. No one else would have made the connection as their name was Jackson, not Baker.

Next, he carefully typed in the details for the 1901 census and looked for no 15 Atlas Street. And there they were, all the family, carefully listed. Below the parents and children, he spotted Hattie's grandfather, George Baker, aged 67, and gave a big grin as he read the occupation, 'puddler'.

I bet not a lot of people can say they've seen one of those at work, he thought to himself. As he gazed at the long, hand-written list, his eyes caught sight of the names belonging to a neighbouring house. A couple of houses away from Hattie's family, there it was....

Mr Michael Baker, miner, aged 66. Beneath his name were listed a wife and eight children. So the skinny little ghost-boy had become a married man and father to all those children!

Because I rescued him.... I really, truly did!

With a huge grin from ear to ear, he asked, "Mum, can we stop at the shop on the way home please? I know now what I have to write in Uncle Freddie's notebook and I think I'm going to need a new pen!"

Notes

The modern Baker family are entirely fictitious. The Baker family in 1900 are *very* loosely based on the family members in the photograph of my Grandmother's family, taken around 1900.

15 Atlas St, Rotherham did exist in 1900 and was the home of the Baker family. It was later demolished.

The Coal Mines Act 1842 banned girls and women, and boys under 10 from working underground in coal mines.

About The Author

 I spent my early life in Rotherham, South Yorkshire, before my parents moved to Lincoln, where I still live, although I am very aware of my Yorkshire roots. My grandmother, one of nine children, had a traditional Victorian childhood in Rotherham, where many of the family were associated with coal mining. Nan would tell us stories about her early life, sometimes sad, often hilarious and I recorded some of our conversations.

Nan died in 1984 aged 96, outliving all the other siblings in the family photograph at the front of this book. But she left us those wonderful rich memories. Although the photograph is real, I have changed the names of most of the characters and other details about them are purely fictional. Much of the background however comes directly from Nan's stories.

I used to teach, and then began working in libraries. Every time a child asked for help with homework on the Victorians I wished I could tell them about Nan's life. One day, while looking closely at the photograph, I realized I could do just that. It occurred to me how close I felt to these people, because of how often Nan had spoken of them. Just suppose a child of today could go back in time and see how their ancestors lived...

And so Charlie Baker was born in my mind, a boy of today, who had the power to travel to any time in history. I hope by introducing other elements very relevant to today's world, this book will appeal to a wide age group and bring the Victorians truly alive to many.

I must thank friends and family, especially my sister, Pam, for her encouragement and my husband, John, for his input and patience when I've been typing for hours on end. Thanks to my grandchildren for correcting me on the speech of today's teenagers and Ellis Delmonte (Hawkwood Books) for advice and help in preparing the book for publication.

Lightning Source UK Ltd.
Milton Keynes UK
UKOW022259241111

182614UK00001B/11/P